"Get Della Street's fingerprints, Paul."

"What?" exclaimed Paul Drake.

"Get Della Street's fingerprints," Mason repeated.

His comely secretary shook her head. "What in the world do you want *my* fingerprints for?"

"I just thought I'd use them in cross-examination. It might have a dramatic effect on the jury."

Drake said, "I don't like this, Perry. You could get into trouble, particularly when you start mixing fingerprints."

Mason looked at him soberly. "I'm in trouble already, Paul."

D0830380

THE CASE OF THE FENCED-IN WOMAN
was originally published by
William Morrow & Company, Inc.

ERLE STANLEY

GARDNER

THE CASE OF THE
FENCED-IN WOMAN

PUBLISHED BY POCKET BOOKS NEW YORK

THE CASE OF THE FENCED-IN WOMAN

William Morrow edition published 1972

POCKET BOOK edition published October, 1973

This POCKET BOOK edition includes every word
contained in the original, higher-priced edition. It is printed
from brand-new plates made from completely reset, clear, easy-to-read
type. POCKET BOOK editions are published by POCKET BOOKS, a division
of Simon & Schuster, Inc., 630 Fifth Avenue, New York, N.Y. 10020.
Trademarks registered in the United States and other countries.

L

Cast of Characters

Publisher's Note

THE MANUSCRIPT for *The Case of the Fenced-In Woman* was one of two full-length Perry Mason novels left in Erle Stanley Gardner's pending file at the time of his death in 1970. Although the work was written a few years earlier and set aside, the publishers believe it was ready for publication. But it should be noted that the author had not done his usual final-draft polishing and checking.

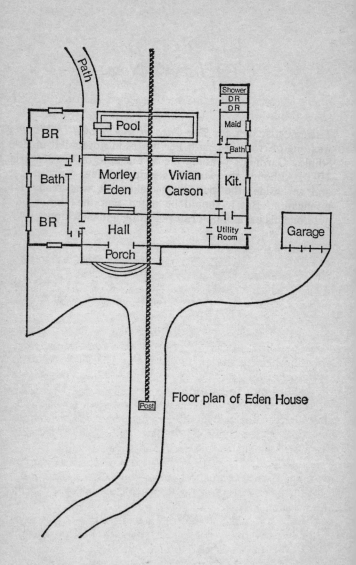

Floor plan of Eden House

Chapter One

PERRY MASON, reading a Supreme Court decision, looked up as Della Street, his confidential secretary, entered the office.

"Della," he said, "endless complications can flow from human conduct. A lawyer never knows what's going to turn up next."

Della Street, a slight smile elevating the corners of her lips, said, "The case of Morley Eden, for instance."

"That's right," Mason said. "Take— *Who* did you say, Della?"

"Morley Eden."

"Eden . . . Eden," Mason repeated thoughtfully. "I don't remember that case. What was it, Della?"

"You haven't heard it yet," Della Street said. "He's waiting in the outer office. He seems to be in quite a predicament."

"What's his trouble?" Mason asked.

"A beautiful woman has run a five-strand barbed-wire fence through the middle of his house," Della Street said.

Mason's eyes searched her. "Is he kidding you, or are you kidding me?" he asked.

"Neither. There's a five-strand barbed-wire fence running directly through his house, with an attractive woman living on the other side of the fence. She apparently has a striking figure, takes sunbaths, but—"

Mason said, "Now that's a situation which illustrates my point. By all means, let's hear the story at firsthand."

"You have an appointment in fifteen minutes," Della Street reminded him.

"That's one client who will have to wait a few minutes," Mason said. "We *must* talk with Morley Eden."

Della Street vanished through the door to the outer office and in a matter of seconds was back, escorting a

1

somewhat stocky individual in his early thirties who was grinning broadly.

"Mr. Mason, Mr. Eden," Della Street said, and moved over to her secretarial chair.

Eden shook hands. "How are you, Mr. Mason? I've heard a lot about you and made up my mind I'd come to you if I was accused of murder. Now I've gone and got myself in a *real* predicament."

Mason said, "I have an appointment in about fifteen minutes. Can you hit the high spots, Mr. Eden?"

"Sure can," Eden said. "Only you're going to cuss me for being so dumb and you'll be a hundred percent right. I brought it all on myself."

Eden sat down in the chair Mason indicated. "It would be funny if it weren't so damned annoying," he said.

Mason passed him a cigarette, took one himself, lit up and said, "Go ahead."

"A fellow by the name of Carson—Loring Carson—had a building site that was a natural for me. It was on two lots he'd bought on speculation for the purpose of putting up a building to sell at a profit. I had a certain type of house I'd designed and this ground had just the right contours ... Now, don't ask me if I'm an architect because I'm not. I'm just a dabbler. I like to dream things up. I became interested in house designing from reading these magazines containing photographs of modern homes —gracious living and all that.

"Carson is a building contractor. He offered me a deal for immediate spot cash that was such a bargain I couldn't resist it. His agreement was to sell me the lots and construct the house to completion within ninety days.

"Now there, of course, is where you're going to start cussing me, and you can't cuss me any more than I've cussed myself. I wanted to get the house started. Loring Carson wanted cash—cash on the barrelhead. I did a quick check and found that part of the property belonged to Loring Carson and part to his wife. I figured he was acting for both of them, so I went ahead with him and he started building. I guess I went ahead too fast."

2

"If the Carsons owned the property free and clear," Mason said, "how does it happen that—"

Eden said, "His wife had filed suit for divorce."

"But if it was community property," Mason said, "the husband is the manager of the property, and if the consideration was adequate . . ."

"That's the whole trouble," Eden said. "It wasn't community property; at least, half of it wasn't. When he bought the property he'd used her separate funds to buy one of the lots and community funds to buy the other. The thing was all mixed up. The judge held one of the two lots was her separate property and the other was community property, which he awarded to Loring Carson as his separate property."

Mason said, "She made no objection when you started building?"

"That's the bad part," Eden said. "I got a letter from her—nicely perfumed stationery—telling me that I was building on her property."

"And what did you do then?"

"Well, I had things started by that time. I asked Carson what he meant by not telling me about the divorce action, and he told me that there was nothing to it, that he had her right where he wanted her, that he'd had a detective on her trail, that she had been stepping out and he had the proof. He said that when he filed his cross-complaint she'd fold up like a blown-out tire. And then he'd deliver me a good deed.

"Well, naturally I just didn't want to take his word for it. I said I wanted to talk with his detective."

"You did?" Mason asked.

"That's right. Fellow by the name of LeGrande Dayton."

"And you were reassured as a result of that conversation?" Mason asked.

"Reassured?" Eden said. "I took one look at the evidence he had and decided Carson was right as rain. I just went ahead and ignored this letter from the wife, Vivian Carson."

"And what happened?" Mason asked.

"Oh, Carson filed his cross-complaint all right, and

3

then they started taking depositions, and then it turned out that this detective had been following the wrong woman. The plan was for Carson to point out his wife so that Dayton could start shadowing her. Carson and Dayton were in a car parked in front of a building where Loring Carson knew his wife was attending a meeting.

"It seems that the women all came out in a group, chatting and laughing. Carson said, 'That's my wife on the edge of the sidewalk, the one in green,' and then ducked down out of sight. What he didn't realize, the way Dayton tells it, is that there were two women in green. Dayton was looking at one, Carson at the other.

"Anyhow, it seems that Dayton started shadowing a woman who was having an affair all right. Dayton got plenty of evidence and reported to Carson he had enough stuff to make winning the case a lead-pipe cinch. Carson filed a cross-complaint. I let Carson go right ahead with my house. Then when they started taking depositions it turned out Carson had got himself on the end of a limb.

"In any event, the judge who tried the case awarded one of the lots to Loring Carson, held that the other one was the separate property of Vivian Carson, his wife, and I'd built my house straddling the two lots.

"Well, of course I thought it would simply be a matter of paying through the nose. I had made a mistake and was willing to pay for it. I sent a representative to Vivian Carson. My agent told her I was sorry about the mix-up, to put a price on her lot . . . Evidently she thought I was all tied in with her husband. She was coldly furious. She told my representative that I could go jump in the lake.

"I felt that if I moved into the house I'd be in possession and then we could work things out some way.

"Well, it seems Vivian Carson is a fighter. She got the judge to issue a restraining order against all persons, her husband or anyone claiming under her husband, from interfering with her possession. When I was away over the weekend she got a surveyor, construction crew and a locksmith. They bored holes in the house right on her side of the boundary line between the two lots, strung barbed wire through the house and pool, and when I came back there she was, living in what she says is her

4

part of the house on one side of the barbed-wire fence, me on the other. She handed me a certified copy of the restraining order and told me she intended to rely upon the very letter of its wording."

"Who was the judge?" Mason asked.

"Judge Hewett L. Goodwin. He's the judge who tried the divorce case."

Mason frowned. "I know Judge Goodwin very well," he said. "He's very conscientious. He tries to decide cases so that the decisions represent substantial justice as between the parties. He gets impatient with technicalities."

"Well," Eden said, "he certainly loused up the job this time."

Mason frowned thoughtfully. "You're married?"

Eden shook his head. "I *was* married. My wife died about three years ago."

"Why did you want to build a house of this sort to live in by yourself?"

"Darned if I know," Eden said. "I like to design things. I like to fool around with a drawing board and pencil. I started designing this house and then it became something of an obsession with me. I simply had to build it and live in it."

"What's your occupation?"

"I guess you'd call me a retired sharpshooter. I made a pretty good wad of dough buying and selling. I like to buy and sell. I'll buy anything that looks good."

"And you'd never met Mrs. Carson but had had all your dealings with her husband?"

"That's right."

"When did you first meet Mrs. Carson?"

"Yesterday," Eden said. "That was Sunday. I came back from a weekend trip and noticed the fence on the outside. I opened the front door, went in and found the barbed wire divided the house. The kitchen door was open and I could see this woman in there cooking, just as calmly and naturally as though she had built the place.

"I guess I stood there with my mouth open. She came walking over to the fence, showed me a certified copy

5

of the restraining order, told me that since we were neighbors she trusted I'd try to cause as little inconvenience as possible and that, as a gentleman, I wouldn't intrude on her privacy. Then she told me she didn't care to have any further conversation and walked away.

"Neighbors!" Eden exclaimed. "I'll tell the world we're neighbors! We're living a cheek-by-jowl existence. When I went out to the swimming pool, there she was in a bikini, taking a sunbath. When I tried to sleep this morning, she was making coffee and the aroma was driving me crazy. I wanted a cup, but she had all the cooking facilities on her side of the house."

"So what happened?" Mason asked.

"Oh, I got up, and I guess she saw from the way I looked that I was dying for a cup of coffee. She asked me if I'd like a cup and I said I would, so she passed me a cup and saucer through the barbed wire and asked me if I liked cream and sugar; said it was just a little neighborly gesture while I was getting settled in my side of the house, that after I'd got settled she didn't care to carry on any further conversations."

Mason smiled and said, "Look, Eden, this is all *too* theatrical. She's simply laying a foundation to get a fancy price for her lot."

"That's the way I felt at first," Eden said. "But now I'm not so sure. That woman is furious. She's mad at her husband for filing that cross-complaint and, as she insists, ruining her reputation. She wants to get even with him in some way.

"I guess Loring Carson was pretty much of a rounder and she evidently had the deadwood on him. He thought *he* was going to get by with it because of the false lead his detective had given him."

Mason pursed his lips. "Mrs. Carson has an attorney, of course, and . . ."

"She says she doesn't," Eden said. "She says she had an attorney to represent her in the divorce action, but as far as her property is concerned, she's going to manage it herself."

"You made overtures about a price?"

6

"I made overtures and got turned down cold and hard."

"And she's a woman who can wear a bikini to advantage?" Mason asked.

"I'll say!" Eden exclaimed. "I understand she was a professional model. How a guy like Carson ever got to first base with her is more than I know. She's *really* class."

Mason glanced over at Della Street, who caught his eye and smiled.

Mason consulted his wristwatch somewhat ruefully. "As I told you, I have an appointment, Eden," he said. "I think I'd better take a look at the premises later on. First, however, I want to talk with Judge Goodwin. I think perhaps we can get him to modify that decree once he understands the facts. I don't suppose that you'll want to try to live there until . . ."

Eden's jaw set belligerently. "Now, that's where I'm going to fool Vivian Carson," he said. "She can't move into my house and dispossess me. I'm going to put in a portable electric grill in the bedroom. My side of the house has a fireplace in it. I'm getting a charcoal grill for the fireplace. I'm going to barbecue steaks, I'm going to fry onions, I'm going to do a little cooking on my own. She has to diet to keep the sort of figure she has. I'll bet the aroma of my cooking will raise hell with her calorie chart."

Mason frowned thoughtfully.

Della Street, turning the pages of Mason's appointment book, said, "Any time after your two-thirty appointment this afterr on. That appointment shouldn't be canceled—you had to cancel it once before. But after that you will have the entire afternoon. You had set that time aside to dictate the brief in the McFarlane case."

"How long will it take me to drive out there?" Mason asked Eden.

"From here, about thirty-five minutes."

Mason looked at his watch. "When a client has an appointment I don't like to keep him waiting," he said. "If you'll just step in the other room with Miss Street, you can draw her a map showing just how to get there. I'll try to be out there late in the afternoon.

7

"In the meantime, Della, call Judge Goodwin's chambers and see if you can make an appointment for the latter part of the afternoon, just as soon as he leaves the bench."

Chapter Two

JUDGE GOODWIN adjourned court shortly before four o'clock and found Perry Mason waiting in the anteroom of his chambers.

"Well, well, well, Counselor," he said, "what brings you here? I've been wondering what you wanted ever since your secretary phoned for an appointment. My work is in the field of domestic relations, while you specialize in murder cases. There shouldn't be any common meeting ground."

"I don't know," Mason said, shaking hands and smiling, "sometimes the alchemy of infatuation leads from blind devotion to homicidal madness."

"Come in," Judge Goodwin said, "and don't discuss such profound truths with a smile."

Judge Goodwin led the way into his chambers and indicated a chair for Mason. Divesting himself of his judicial robe, he settled down with a sigh, offered the lawyer a cigarette, took one himself and said, "I suppose there's a polarization of sex magnetism that causes physical proximity to change the . . . Oh well, you didn't come here to discuss that, despite the fact you opened up the subject. What's on your mind?"

"The case of Vivian Carson versus Loring Carson," Mason said. "Do you remember it?"

A smile twisted Judge Goodwin's lips. "I remember it *very* well indeed."

"You made a peculiar order in that case."

"Did I? What's peculiar about it?"

"You decided that a certain portion of real property belonged to Vivian Carson as her sole and separate property, that the adjoining property was community property which you awarded to Loring Carson."

Judge Goodwin said, "I did that deliberately and with a definite objective in mind."

"A short time ago," Mason said, studying the judge's face, "you signed an order restraining Loring Carson or his agents or assigns from interfering in any way with the property awarded Vivian Carson as her separate property."

Judge Goodwin smiled. "I remember signing the restraining order very well indeed."

Mason said, "The situation is complicated, Judge, because my client, Morley Eden, has a house he purchased from Loring Carson. It's on both lots.

"After your restraining order was issued, Vivian Carson had a surveyor run the line of the property, bore holes in the house and run a barbed-wire fence completely through the house, dividing it into two portions and dividing the front and back of the property, including the swimming pool, as well."

Judge Goodwin smoked in silence for a few seconds, then his smile broadened into a grin. "Did she actually do that?" he asked.

"She did just that," Mason said. "And, what's more, she's living in her side of the house and Morley Eden is living in his side of the house."

"An opportunity to be real neighborly," Judge Goodwin said.

"Except for the barbed-wire fence," Mason pointed out.

Judge Goodwin ground out the cigarette in an ashtray and pursed his lips thoughtfully.

"Knowing your ideas of doing substantial justice, and your impatience with the technicalities of the law which at times tend to thwart real justice," Mason went on, "I was interested to find out just what caused the decision and to see if it wouldn't be possible to modify it."

"To modify it in what way?" Judge Goodwin asked.

"So that Loring Carson could be awarded the entire

9

property and the rights of Vivian Carson could be protected by disposition of some other property."

Judge Goodwin said, "Mason, you know my feeling about the law. You know my feeilng about the responsibility of being a judge called upon to determine the right and wrong in human disputes.

"Now, I'm going to tell you something in confidence. I knew all about the situation when I signed that restraining order. Morley Eden is, as you know, a wealthy man and an impulsive man. He's a square shooter but impulsive.

"Now then, when Eden first dealt with Carson on that property, I'm satisfied that Loring Carson made some false representations about the evidence of his wife's infidelity.

"If Eden had been a poor man, I might have felt differently about it. But as for Loring Carson, Carson felt —to use a popular expression—that he had this court over a barrel, that the court didn't dare do anything except affirm the transaction.

"Loring Carson has proven himself to be a thorough-going heel. He hired a detective who may or may not have been acting in good faith, but in any event he shadowed the wrong individual. However, before that became clear, his wife's good name was blasted to shreds. The charges against her made headlines, were bandied about by gossipmongers and unquestionably did a lot to embarrass Vivian Carson.

"The husband has absolutely no regrets about this at all. He simply says it was the detective's mistake and washes his hands of the whole matter.

"I'm satisfied Eden has a cause of action against Loring Carson for willful fraud. I'm hoping that the situation reaches the point where Eden is forced into filing an action of fraud against Carson. Frankly, I'd like to see Carson pay through the nose."

"It isn't that simple," Mason said. "My client had that house designed to his own specifications. The building site was one that he wanted above all others. He might sue Carson for fraud, but he'd want to continue to live there."

"Then let him live there."

"But that brings up an embarrassing situation with Vivian Carson."

"Then let him buy her out."

"Apparently," Mason said, "Vivian Carson is downright good and mad. She doesn't want to sell to anyone. She doesn't want to do anything that is going to get her husband off the spot or help her husband's purchaser in any way."

"And I don't blame her in the least," Judge Goodwin said. "Of course, Mason, you know and I know that when a marriage breaks up it quite frequently is six of one and half a dozen of the other. The man may be the one who commits the first sin, but as the relationship deteriorates the woman has a tendency to retaliate.

"Or, on the other hand, if the woman starts nagging, the man quite speedily loses interest and begins stepping out with someone who meets him on an amorous plane.

"I'm not dumb enough or naïve enough to believe that in all these marriage failures the fault is entirely on one side, because I've seen enough of human nature to know that it isn't. But I do know that in this case Loring Carson was a heel. I know that he is a fast-talking, sharp-shooting individual who's after a quick buck, and that whenever he gets in a corner he starts pulling a razzle-dazzle.

"He not only gravely wronged his wife and shows no regret for having done so, but he tried to pull some financial sleight of hand on this court. He's managed things so it's impossible to trace his cash assets. Too much cash has disappeared. He says he had heavy losses on the gambling tables at Las Vegas.

"The evidence shows that he went to Las Vegas frequently. He was interested in one of the hostesses there, a young woman named Genevieve Honcutt Hyde. Apparently he became intimate with this woman. I don't hold that against him too much because by that time his marriage had deteriorated to a cat-and-dog existence. But I don't think Carson lost anywhere near as much as he claims. I think Carson has been using Las Vegas as a means of confusing his assets, and I think that for

11

the past year he's been taking large sums of money and concealing it.

"Now I wouldn't confess this to anyone whom I didn't know and admire, but I'm going to tell you, Perry Mason, that I just decided to let Morley Eden take on Loring Carson for a while."

Mason regarded the jurist thoughtfully. "It is almost as if Mrs. Carson had been reading your mind."

"Yes?" Judge Goodwin asked.

"She seems to be utilizing the situation for all it is worth. For instance, I understand she put on a very abbreviated bikini and took occasion to take a sunbath on her half of the swimming pool while my client was inspecting the barbed-wire division."

"And your client objected to that?" Judge Goodwin asked, smiling.

"Well, it made an embarrassing situation."

"Embarrassing for whom?"

"Generally embarrassing," Mason said.

"Vivian Carson is a very attractive woman," Judge Goodwin said. "She was, I understand, a highly successful model before she was married. She's doubtless been seen in a bikini before. I doubt if she was embarrassed."

Mason said, "It makes the grass on the other side of the fence look rather green to a bachelor, and that may be what she has in mind."

"That may well be," Judge Goodwin said, "but let's not have any misunderstanding, Mr. Mason. If your client so much as sticks a finger through that fence or does anything to invade the premises on the other side of the property line, the court will consider that conduct a violation of the restraining order.

"After all, your client is an assignee of Loring Carson. He's claiming title under Loring Carson. Very frankly, and off the record, I hope to see Loring Carson suffer just as much inconvenience as possible, because I want to see him pay through the nose. I think he has been milking cash out of his income for some time and concealing it. I think he has been cheating the Internal Revenue Service and I think he has been concealing his true financial status from his wife. I doubt if his wife

12

can hire detectives and smoke out the facts, but if your client gets mad enough, I think he'll get a judgment against Carson and then I think he'll be man enough to find these hidden assets. When he does that, I'll reopen proceedings on the property division and reapportion the community property.

"Now that may or may not be good law, but it's good psychology. It *may* teach Loring Carson that he can't pull a financial razzle-dazzle on this court and then stand back and laugh about it."

"It's an intriguing situation," Mason said, eyeing Judge Goodwin shrewdly. "When the newspaper reporters get hold of it, it's certainly good for a feature story."

Judge Goodwin nodded, then grinned.

"Damn it," Mason charged, "you engineered this whole thing. You knew exactly what was going to happen and you're sitting back there and enjoying it."

Judge Goodwin said, "When I sit as a judge in a case I try to do substantial justice between the parties. I can only make decrees, and decrees are simply pieces of paper. I have, however, made a judgment in this case which I think will *eventually* get results."

Mason got to his feet. "All right, Your Honor," he said, bowing. "And keeping my remarks off the record, I can assure you that your judgment has raised hell."

Judge Goodwin said, "If you are waiting to hear any expressions of regret from me, Mason, you'll have to wait a lot longer than I'm going to be here."

Chapter Three

MASON RANG his office and, when the switchboard operator answered, said, "Let me talk with Della Street."

A moment later his secretary came on the line and he said, "Judge Goodwin is sympathetic to our client but just as firm as a brick wall as far as his decision is concerned, Della. He says that Loring Carson is a heel and the best way he can reach Carson is through a decision of this sort. He's hoping that our client, Morley Eden, will proceed to put Loring Carson through a meat grinder."

"And so?" Della asked.

"So," Mason said, "I am going out and look the premises over. I just wanted to let you know there's no need for you to wait."

"Isn't it a little late for that?"

"What do you mean, Della?"

"The ex-model in the bikini will probably be well finished with her sunbath."

Mason laughed. "She might be in an attractive skintight cocktail gown by this time."

"How delightful," Della Street said. "You can have a neighborly chat, with cocktails served through a five-strand barbed-wire fence. Be careful you don't get scratched."

"I'll do that," Mason said. "Button up the office for the night, Della. Give Morley Eden a ring and tell him I'm on my way out."

Following the sketch map his client had given Della, Mason came at last to a road which wound through rolling hills to end on a natural plateau beyond which there was a drop-off into a little valley purpled with the rays of the declining sun.

The house was a long, low structure with artificially weathered thick shingles. It had the appearance of having aged naturally and blended perfectly with the surroundings.

The driveway which approached the house was bisected by a five-strand barbed-wire fence, anchored to a concrete post in the middle of the driveway.

Mason took the left-hand drive, noticing as he did so that the parking place, most of which was on the right-hand side of the barbed-wire fence, was well filled with cars.

As Mason brought his car to a stop in front of sweeping semicircular steps leading to the front door, Morley Eden, who had evidently been watching the driveway, opened the door and walked across the broad porch area to greet the lawyer.

"Believe it or not," Eden said, "they're having a party, and it's the damnedest party you ever saw."

"What's wrong with it?"

"There isn't a man in the place; just a flock of good-looking women. From the looks of them I'd say they were all models. Perfect figures, snaky gowns that cling like the skin on a sausage."

"They're talking with you?" Mason asked.

"Not a word. They're waiting for me to break the ice, I guess."

"You break the ice and you'll land in jail," Mason said. "This whole thing is an elaborate trap. Technically you are claiming under Loring Carson. Therefore you come within the provisions of the restraining order relating to his agents and assigns. If you interfere in any way with the possession of that other side of the house, your goose is cooked. That's why Vivian Carson is bringing out all this tempting array of feminine pulchritude. She hopes that you'll be encouraged to take the initiative and make a pass."

"I gathered as much," Eden said, "but this is the sort of torture a man can't endure very long."

"Check out, then, and go to a hotel," Mason said.

Eden's jaw clamped shut. "I'll be damned if I will! I'll fight it out with her on these grounds if it takes all winter. Come on in and take a look."

Eden held the door open. Mason entered a reception hall, walked through an arched doorway which could be shut off from the reception hall by heavy draperies and down three steps to a living room. It was sumptuously furnished and lighted by concealed lights which gave the room an atmosphere of soft moonlight.

About one-third of the room was separated by the taut strands of the barbed-wire fence, which ran in a mathematically straight line directly through the house and through the wall. Above it stretched a rod.

On the other side of the fence a group of women, seemingly oblivious to their unusual surroundings, were having cocktails and chatting gaily, their voices at times

15

rising to a crescendo of rapid communication which indicated the liquid in the cocktail glasses had plenty of alcoholic content.

Apparently no one noticed Mason entering the room and no one paid the slightest attention to Morley Eden as he stood and gestured with his hand. "There you are," he said.

Mason walked over to the barbed-wire fence, a quizzical smile on his face. He planted his feet far apart, pushed his hands down into his coat pockets and surveyed the spectacle.

Abruptly one of the young women, a vivacious redhead with dancing blue eyes, saw Perry Mason, stopped in her tracks, did a quick double take, then came over to the barbed-wire fence. "Well, *what* do you know?" she said. "Aren't you Perry Mason, the lawyer?"

Mason nodded.

"Well, for heaven sakes, fancy seeing *you* here! What in the world *are* you doing here?"

"Right at the moment," Mason said, "I'm advising a client. Now may I ask what you're doing here?"

"Just finishing my second cocktail and thinking about a third," the young woman said. "Only I'm giving the matter the benefit of mature consideration because I have trouble retracting my landing gear when I get loaded."

"And may I ask what's the occasion for all this?" Mason asked.

"Heavens, I don't know," she said. "Vivian told us to put on skin-tight dresses and abbreviated lingerie we could show to advantage.

"It seems somebody connected with her ex-husband lives in the other part of the house. We're supposed to report any passes that he might make."

"So far, no passes?" Mason asked.

She laughed. "The evening's young yet. He—"

"Helene, *what* are you doing?" a woman asked, striding over to the fence.

The redhead giggled. "Talking with Perry Mason," she said.

"I told you not to make any leads."

"Oh, go roll a hoop," the young woman said. "Your

caution was related to the guy who's tied up with your ex-husband. This is Perry Mason, the lawyer. Don't you know him? Good heavens, I've been a fan of his forever. Fancy actually *meeting* you, Mr. Mason."

Mason said to the other woman, "I presume you're Vivian Carson."

She studied him thoughtfully and said, "That's right. May I ask what you're doing here?"

"Making a survey of the situation."

"All right," Mrs. Carson said, "Helene has spoiled the act. I . . ."

"You were setting a trap?" Mason asked, as she hesitated.

Abruptly her eyes softened. "Frankly, Mr. Mason," she said, "I . . . Well, I don't think I'm going to make any admissions."

"I was just trying to get oriented," Mason said. "I wouldn't try to discuss things with you in the absence of your attorney."

She said, "I'm representing myself. I suppose that means I have a fool for a client, but my attorney didn't approve of the things I had in mind."

"Were they that bad?" Mason asked.

"They were worse . . . Now I see your client inching his way over here, hoping to get into the conversation. I'd advise you to keep him out of it."

"Why?" Mason asked. "You've already broken the ice giving him coffee—remember?"

"Of course I remember, and for your personal, private and confidential information, Mr. Mason, that was a part of my act. Even the most hardy soul can't withstand the aroma of coffee in the morning.

"Under the law, as I understand it, the initiative is mine. When I want to talk with your client, I'll talk. But he can't take the initiative and talk with me or with my guests.

"The minute he does anything other than leer, I'm going to nail him for contempt of court."

"Do you hate him that much?"

"I hate my husband that much, and that's the only

17

way I can get even with him and get the sort of action I want."

Morley Eden, approaching Mason, said, "Pardon me, Perry, but I—"

"Just a minute," Mason said, motioning him to silence.

"I thought," Eden insisted, "that since *you* apparently were getting acquainted I might at least talk to you."

Mason, his eyes twinkling said, "Oh, it's quite all right to talk to *me*. This is *your* house on *your* property and you can talk to anyone on *your* side of the fence."

Eden said, "You might advise the young woman that while the legal difficulties are being adjusted I'd like to live in harmony."

Mason turned to Mrs. Carson and said, "Mrs. Carson, my client wishes me to assure you that he has no hard feelings."

"You might also explain to her," Eden said, "that the pleasure which is afforded a lonely man of seeing a young woman with Mrs. Carson's grace disporting herself around the swimming pool more than compensates for the inconvenience of the barbed-wire fence through my living room. You might also tell her that any time she would like to dive under the barbed wire and use the springboard at my end of the pool I'd be only too glad to have her."

Vivian Carson looked him over with appraising eyes, abruptly turned to Perry Mason and said, "I think you'd better advise your client, Mr. Mason, that any attempt to fraternize with the enemy will be regarded as a contempt of court."

"Please tell her," Eden said hastily, "that I don't regard her as an enemy and I don't want to regard her as an enemy. I can appreciate what she's trying to do and I can appreciate something of the injustice that has been done her."

Vivian Carson started to turn away, then whirled with an impulsive gesture graceful as that of a dancer. She extended her hand through the barbed wire and said, "I'm sorry. Mr. Eden. You're a good sort. I've been trying to make things as difficult for you as possible and you've been nice about it."

Eden took her hand, said, "Thank you, Mrs. Carson.

18

I take it it's all right to shake hands as long as it's *your* hand that's on *my* side of the fence."

"Exactly," Vivian said, smiling, "and now, having acted on impulse, I've ruined a good part of my scheme. But I'm warning you, Morley Eden, I'm going to get back at my husband for the things he's done, and, as it happens, you're in the line of fire."

"I take it," Mason said, "this little exchange of pleasantries is not going to be reported to the court."

"What's the use?" she said. "I led with my chin. I was the one who broke the ice. You *do* have awfully nice clients, Mr. Mason; but this fence is going to stay up, and I trust that in the course of time Mr. Eden will be so inconvenienced by the things that go on here he will take drastic action."

"With wire cutters?" Mason asked.

"I don't care what sort of action he takes. Whatever he does is going to be a violation of the restraining order, and once this temporary truce is over, Mr. Eden, I warn you that making any passes at my friends on this side of the fence is going to be considered a violation of the court's order."

"It's an embarrassing situation," Eden said. "I know now something of the tortures of Tantalus."

"You haven't seen anything yet," she said. "Wait until . . . Well, just wait."

"I'll live through it," Eden promised.

"My client," Mason said gravely, "has plans to install an electric organ. He'll play a lot at night."

"Oh, that will be just dandy!" Vivian Carson said, her eyes sparkling, "because I've arranged to take cornet lessons and my teacher plays in an orchestra. He told me he could only come at unconventional times, and I told him I was certain that would be all right."

"I think," Eden said, wincing, "it might be a good plan if we dispensed with the music, Mrs. Carson, and just went at it hammer and tongs."

"Hammer and tongs it is," she said, giving him her hand once more. "Come on, Helene."

Helene pushed her hand through the barbed wire. "I'm

19

being paged, Mr. Mason. But it certainly was nice to see you."

"Perhaps," Mason told her, "we'll meet again when the barriers are not so sharply drawn or so effectively patroled."

"I'm for that," she said. "Perhaps we could ride fence together."

"Perhaps," Mason said.

Vivian Carson gently but firmly took her arm and drew her away.

Mason said, "Judge Goodwin is determined to force Loring Carson into making a more complete disclosure of certain community assets. He's hoping that you'll sue for fraud."

"Should I?" Eden asked.

"I think you should."

"Go ahead and sue him then," Eden said. "File suit for all the damages you think you can recover. Pile it on just as thick as the traffic will stand."

"Lawsuits take time and money," Mason said.

"Shorten the time. I've got the money. You go ahead and—"

Chimes sounded.

"Someone at the front door," Eden said.

Mason said, "I suggest you close the curtains in the arched doorway before answering the chimes."

"I'll do that," Eden said, "but the curtain won't shut out the sounds."

Left alone in the divided living room, Mason sank into a comfortable chair and watched the party going on on the other side of the barbed-wire fence.

Mason heard Vivian Carson say, "All right, girls. We're going to model the lingerie for Mrs. Sterling."

There was a spatter of applause.

An older woman, stepping forward, said, "I'll warn you I'm going to be difficult to sell. I want something that's lacy, distinctive and . . . saucy."

Two of the young women wheeled a dais from a corner of the room, then brought out some movable steps. Vivian Carson switched on a spotlight which played on the dais in the center.

The model who had been addressed as Helene came forward and stood up on the dais.

"May I have your attention, girls?" she said. "First I'm going to show you what I've got on. I think it's sufficiently . . . well, saucy."

She reached for the zipper of her dress.

Mason noticed that Vivian Carson had moved quietly and unostentatiously to the perimeter of the watching circle, that her eyes were darting in a swift survey of Morley Eden's portion of the living room.

Mason, moving over to the fence, said, "I don't like to mention it, Mrs. Carson, but your pigeon has flown the coop."

"What do you mean?"

"Morley Eden isn't here."

"Morley Eden has nothing to do with it," she said.

Helene slipped the dress off her shoulders, let it drop to the floor and stepped out of it.

The spotlight outlined her superb figure, arrayed in a perfectly fitted slip.

A voice said, "Now this number is thirteen twenty-six. You'll notice the scallops around the lower edge and——"

From the outer hallway came the unmistakable sound of a blow and a thud.

Mason hurried through the heavy curtains to find Morley Eden sprawled on the floor. A younger, athletic individual, his face contorted with emotion, stood over the sprawled figure.

Eden said, "Why, you . . . you . . . I'll . . ."

He started scrambling to his feet.

The other man braced himself.

"Here, wait a minute," Mason said. "What goes on here?"

"He hit me," Eden said.

"And I'm going to hit you again," the man said. "Get up and take it."

Mason pushed himself between the two men. "Now, wait a minute," he said. "What's all this about?"

"You keep out of this," the man said, "unless you want some of the same."

21

"All right," Mason told him, "if *that's* the way you feel about it, I'll take some of the same."

The man sized up Mason's broad shoulders, granite-hard features, and hesitated. Then sudden recognition supplanted the rage in his eyes. "Why, you're the lawyer!" he exclaimed. "You're Perry Mason!"

"That's right, I'm Perry Mason. Now, what's this all about?"

Behind the lawyer, Eden, scrambling to his feet, said, "Let him try hitting me when I'm expecting it. Let him . . ."

Mason, keeping his body between the two men, said to Eden over his shoulder, "Just calm down a minute, Eden. Let's find out what this is all about."

"I'll tell you what it's all about," Eden said. "He thinks I'm Loring Carson and—"

"You're *not?*" the man exclaimed.

"That man," Mason said, "is Morley Eden. Now, who are you and what do you want?"

"Morley Eden! But . . . what's *he* doing here?"

"For your information, he bought this property from Loring Carson. Now, who are you and what do you want?"

"My gosh, I'm sorry," the man said. "I . . . I guess my temper has run away with me again."

"I guess it has," Mason said. "Now what's this all about?"

"I'm Norbert Jennings. He knows who I am."

"I know who you are simply as a name," Eden said, moving around to flank Mason.

The lawyer, seeing there was no indication that hostilities would be resumed immediately, said, "All right, let's get this straight. Just how do you enter into this picture, Mr. Jennings?"

"Your client will know," Jennings said sullenly.

Eden said, "Norbert Jennings was the man Loring Carson named in his cross-complaint as having an affair with Vivian Carson."

"I see," Mason said.

"You don't see anything," Jennings said. "That man

22

ruined me. He and his damned tin-star, gumshoe private eye."

"He was following you?" Mason asked.

"He was following Nadine Palmer," Jennings said.

"It was all a mistake," Eden interposed. "Carson was supposed to put the finger on his wife for LeGrande Dayton, the detective. But the detective became confused and thought that Mrs. Palmer was the one he was to follow."

"That's the story now," Jennings said. "They've certainly messed up *my* life."

"What happened?" Mason asked.

"What happened!" Jennings said. "They smeared my name all over the court records."

"Did it get in the papers?"

"Of course it did. I'm the prize fall guy of the year. They laugh at me at the club, at the golf course, everywhere. It's getting so I don't like to go out."

"And Nadine Palmer's husband?"

"She hasn't any. They're divorced," Jennings said. "All right, we were interested in each other. I was meeting her at various places. Don't tell me I shouldn't, because I am not in the mood to have anyone start preaching."

"You're not *married?*" Mason asked.

"No."

"Then what are you kicking about?"

"Because that guy, Carson, made me a laughingstock. Getting caught was bad enough. The word was spread around that I'd been stepping out with Vivian Carson. Then it turned out that it was all a mistake and it wasn't Vivian Carson at all, but Nadine Palmer.

"That made a funny story out of it. No one ever lives down a funny story. Everybody's laughing at the story and sympathizing with her, and a woman of her caliber can't stand sympathy.

"I came here to tell Loring Carson just what a heel he was. This man opened the door, asked me what I wanted and I told him who I was and then he acted dumb. I guess I got mad. I mean, I *was* mad. I let my temper get the best of me."

23

Eden said, "You sneaked that punch in on me. You . . ."

"I didn't sneak anything," Jennings said. "After you've named a man as corespondent in a cross-complaint you ought to be expecting a sock in the puss."

"But I didn't name anybody as corespondent."

Jennings slowly grinned. "All right, I'll apologize," he said. "Now then, you've got a lawyer here. You tell me how much damages you want for that sock on the puss and I'll write you a check, and my apologies go with the check."

Eden thought things over.

"Well?" Mason prompted.

Eden grinned ruefully, rubbed his jaw. "When you put it that way," he said, "I guess I don't want anything. I can see things from your viewpoint. You aren't half as mad at Loring Carson as I am. When you see him, just pass on that sock on the jaw to him and then give him another one for me."

"I'll see him all right," Jennings promised grimly. "The dirty bounder!"

"And how about Nadine Palmer?" Mason asked. "How is she taking all this?"

"I wouldn't know. Every time I try to call her she hangs up on me."

"You tried to see her after that?" Mason asked.

"I did see her after that, but we didn't go out together. If we had, every gossip columnist in the city would have had a field day writing those tongue-in-cheek articles about the woman in green."

"May I ask what you discussed with her, generally?" Mason asked.

"You may not. It's none of your damn business."

"Of course," Mason pointed out, "if she is no longer married . . ."

"She's a darn nice girl," Norbert Jennings interposed angrily, "and don't pull any of that line with me. She's human and she has human feelings, and she has pride and she has her good name. She's always been tremendously popular and now whenever she walks into a room eye-

24

brows start lifting . . . Damn Carson! If I ever get my hands on him I'll . . . I'll . . ."

"Take it easy," Mason said. "Making threats can sometimes be an expensive luxury."

"All right," Jennings said. "I've got money. I can afford to pay for the luxuries I want. Making threats happens at the moment to be a luxury that interests me. I'll repeat. If I ever get my hands on Loring Carson I'm going to make that yellow-livered cur whimper for mercy. I'm going to . . ."

"Perhaps you have legal redress," Mason said.

"Legal redress, my eye. I could sue the louse and what good would that do? In the first place if he had any money I wouldn't want it. Every nickel that I'd get from him would be money I wouldn't touch with a ten-foot pole. What's more, you can't get blood out of a turnip."

"Have you considered the possibility that he may have money cached away?" Mason asked.

"I tell you, I'm not interested in money," Norbert Jennings said angrily. "I've *got* money! I've got all the money I want. I've got too damned much money. It's never given me any happiness yet. I . . . To hell with it . . . I'm sorry, Eden. I guess you're on the receiving end of this the same way I am. I'm really sorry I socked you."

He pushed forward an impulsive hand.

Eden took it.

Without another word, Jennings turned and left the house.

"Well," Eden said, rubbing his jaw, "we keep getting into more and more complications."

Mason said, "I might also advise you that a Mrs. Sterling, who seems to be buyer for some feminine establishment, is having a lingerie-modeling session in your fenced-off living room."

"The devil," Eden said, grinning. "I suppose this was all arranged."

"I suppose so," Mason said.

"How far had it gone?"

"The first model was wearing the lingerie. She did a species of striptease on a raised dais and—"

25

"Well, well, well," Eden interrupted, "perhaps the situation will have some advantages after all."

"Now wait a minute," Mason said, "no matter how you figure this thing, it's bait, and while I don't know where the hook is right now, don't take the bait."

"You mean, don't look?" Eden asked.

"Well," Mason said, grinning, "I guess we'll have to look."

"Exactly," Eden said. "Acting purely and professionally as my attorney, I see you're going to have to prolong your visit. All right, let's go."

Eden pulled back the drapes on the doorway, disclosing the living room.

On the other side of the barbed-wire fence on the dais a beautiful model, attired in lingerie, was pirouetting slowly.

Standing at one corner of the room, Vivian Carson was watching, not the model but the arched doorway.

The minute Mason and Eden entered the room Vivian Carson grasped the edge of a piece of cloth, nodded to a young woman standing at the opposite end of the room from her and they advanced toward each other, pulling and tugging at improvised curtains which, after sticking a time or two, were pulled together to close off that section of the living room.

"So *that's* the reason she put up a rod above the barbed-wire fence," Eden said.

Mason grinned. "It seems she thinks of everything," he said.

"So it would seem," Eden observed. "And I suppose if I so much as put a finger on the other side of that barbed-wire fence to widen the gap between the two sections of cloth I'd . . ."

"Be guilty of contempt of court," Mason finished.

Eden sighed. "Well, I guess the only thing to do now is to find a nightclub with a good striptease."

"And, under the circumstances," Mason said, "it would seem that I have nothing more to discuss with you."

Eden laughed. "One question, Mason."

"What?"

"If that curtain hadn't been there and the lingerie

show had continued, would you have billed me for your time while you sat watching the show?"

"Sure I would," Mason said. "That comes under the heading of 'conference with a client.' "

"I can see I've taken up the wrong profession." Eden grinned. "What the hell do you suppose that woman will think of next?"

"That," Mason said, "is something I'm not even going to try to predict. I'll have a complaint ready for you to verify in a fraud action day after tomorrow. Come to the office around ten to sign the papers. Then we'll try to serve them on Carson."

Chapter Four

PERRY MASON, pacing the floor of his office, paused to look out of the window at the morning sunlight, consulted his wristwatch, turned impatiently to Della Street.

"How's the fraud complaint coming, Della?"

"The typist will have it ready in fifteen minutes."

"I want to file it as soon after ten o'clock as possible," Mason said. "How about Paul Drake? Hasn't he come in yet?"

"Apparently not. He was working on a case until all hours this morning and I left word for him to get in touch with you just as soon as he came in."

"Well, that's the worst of running a detective agency," Mason said. "You can't plan your time, but just the same I—"

He broke off as knuckles sounded in code sequence on the corridor door of the private office.

"That's Paul now. Let him in, will you please, Della?"

Della Street opened the door.

Paul Drake, head of the Drake Detective Agency, looking worn and haggard, said, "Hi, folks. It's a beautiful morning for this time of year, isn't it? That is, if you care for beautiful mornings and this time of year."

"We care," Mason said.

"I was afraid you would. Personally, I'm past caring. What gives?"

Mason said, "A little after ten o'clock this morning, Paul, I'm going to be filing a complaint in a case entitled Morley Eden versus Loring Carson. It's going to be quite a complaint."

"A civil action?" Drake asked.

"That's right. It's an action on the ground of fraud. Loring Carson claimed that he could guarantee title to certain property, that he had evidence which would defeat his wife's divorce action, that he could prove her guilty of infidelity and that two lots of real estate were community property, that she had no separate property rights in any of the real estate."

"And that was all false?" Drake asked.

"Was it false!" Mason said. "You don't know the half of it. Apparently Carson was lying about the whole setup. In addition to that, he either deliberately or accidentally steered his private detective onto another woman in place of his wife. The indiscretions of this other woman were duly chronicled in Carson's cross-complaint in the divorce action as being those of Mrs. Carson. Moreover, there seems to be a pretty general feeling that he has money stashed away somewhere in the form of cash. Evidently he has seen this coming for some time and he was getting ready to clean up and skip out if he had to.

"Judge Hewitt L. Goodwin, before whom the divorce case was tried, feels pretty much worked up about this and would like to get at the bottom of it. He'd dearly love to find where Carson has money hidden."

"So you're filing a complaint on the ground of fraud?"

"That's right," Mason said. "And I'm going to follow that up with a request to take Carson's deposition. I'm going to examine him about certain matters under oath. I'm particularly interested in any hidden assets in the form of concealed cash."

"And what do you want *me* to do?"

"For one thing," Mason said, "I want you to locate

28

Carson. Later on I'll want you to put a shadow on him. In case he has any tendency to skip out after the papers are served on him I'd like to know where he's going in case he should take to the tall timber.

"I particularly want to find out all I can about his background so that I will have questions to ask on the deposition that will make it difficult for him to lie."

"Such as what?"

"Such as where he's been living; whether he's ever used any other names; whether he has any other bank accounts under different names; whether he has any safety-deposit boxes; things of that sort.

"Moreover, it seems Carson has a girl friend who's a hostess at one of the night spots in Las Vegas. Her name is Genevieve Honcutt Hyde, and Carson has been seeing a lot of her. He's used this Las Vegas background to support his claim that he's been losing heavily at the tables.

"Judge Goodwin, however, feels Carson has been getting his assets in the form of cash and concealing them somewhere. We have to find out."

"That stuff's virtually impossible to get at," Drake said.

"You've had a hard night?" Mason asked.

"I've had a hard night and a hard morning," Drake agreed, smiling ruefully. "I got to bed about three o'clock. It certainly seemed that the sun moved around mighty fast; but even if I did have a hard night, that Las Vegas stuff is hard enough to get to justify my pessimism. Okay, Perry, I'll see what I can do. Where can I find this Carson, do you know?"

Before Mason could answer the question the telephone bell on Della Street's desk jangled. She picked up the phone, said, "Yes, Gertie . . . What? . . . Who? . . . You mean Loring Carson? . . . Just a minute, Gertie."

Della Street put her hand over the mouthpiece of the phone and said, "Mr. Loring Carson is in the office and wants to see you at once upon a matter of the greatest importance."

Mason grinned. "Speaking of angels," he said, "we hear the flutter of their wings. Just stand in the doorway, Paul, and be taking leave as Carson comes in. That will give you a chance to see him. After that you'll be able to recognize him."

"That," Drake said, "will also give him a chance to see me. If you don't mind, Perry, I'll case him from the hall when he leaves. Just be sure that he goes out this door and when he leaves be sure to say, 'Well, good day, Mr. Carson,' or 'I'm afraid that's all I can do for you, Mr. Carson,' or something of the sort. Mention his name."

Mason nodded, said to Della Street, "Go out and escort Mr. Carson into the office, will you please, Della?"

Paul Drake slipped silently through the exit door to the corridor.

Della returned after a moment, holding the door open to admit a chunky man with an aggressive personality who came barging forward with hand outstretched.

"*Mr.* Mason!" he said.

Mason bowed and after a moment accepted the outstretched hand.

"I'm Loring Carson. My ears have been burning a bit. Guess you think I'm pretty much of a heel, eh?"

"I don't know that my personal opinion has anything to do with it, Mr. Carson. I think I should tell you that I am representing interests that are adverse to yours, and those interests will take such steps as are deemed necessary by me in order to protect themselves."

Carson laughed. "That's certainly a diplomatic way of putting it, Mr. Mason. Suppose you and I have a little talk and at the end of that time perhaps you won't feel like taking this action you're talking about."

"I don't think I should talk with you," Mason said. "You are an adverse party and if you don't have an attorney representing you at the present time it's going to be necessary for you to get one. I'm willing to talk with your attorney, but not with you."

"Oh, phooey with all that professional ethics business," Carson said. "I'm the captain of the ship. If I get an attorney he'll do what I tell him to."

"I still don't want to talk with you," Mason said.

"You aren't going to try to throw me out, are you?"

"I might," Mason said.

"Well, unless you do throw me out I'm going to talk with you. As a matter of fact I haven't any attorney. My attorney quit me in a huff. Said that I'd misled him and got him into an impossible position."

"I see," Mason said noncommittally.

"As a matter of fact it wasn't anything of the sort," Carson went on. "The whole trouble was with that stupid private detective I hired. Man by the name of LeGrande Dayton. And if he's a detective, I'm a nursemaid's aunt.

"He wanted me to point my wife out to him. Naturally you can't walk up with a private detective, point your finger and say, 'That's the woman right there. Hello, honey, how are you?' And then your wife will say, 'Well, what's this all about? Who's this man you got with you?' And you say, 'Oh, he's just a guy—someone that wanted to know what you looked like so I told him I'd point you out.' "

Carson threw back his head and laughed.

"You have to handle these things judiciously, Mason. I told this detective to shadow the one in dark green just coming out of the door; the one on the edge of the sidewalk. Then I ducked down behind the seat. Well, naturally I meant the inside edge of the sidewalk. He thought that I meant the woman who was on the outside edge of the sidewalk—at least that's what he says now."

"And he shadowed the wrong woman?" Mason asked.

"That's right. Went ahead and got all the dope on her. He asked me if I wanted to break a door down and take pictures and I decided I didn't want to go that strong. That's where I made my big mistake—I'd have found it was the wrong person. But he had all the affidavits, photostats of registrations at the motel and all of that, and I went along for the ride—and believe me, they took me for a ride."

Mason said, "I still don't care to discuss matters with you, Mr. Carson. You're going to need an attorney."

Carson said, "I don't need any lawyer. I sympathize with Eden. Everything I told him I told him in good faith. There wasn't any fraud connected with it. There

31

wasn't any breach of trust. Morley and I were dealing at arm's length."

"I don't care to discuss it with you," Mason said.

"You're not discussing it with me; I'm discussing it with you. Now, I'm just going to tell you something, Mr. Mason. You just sit back on this thing and hold your horses. I'll get it straightened out, but I don't want you filing any suit charging me with fraud or anything of that sort. You get that now, that's important. I'm in a position right at the moment where I'm conducting some delicate negotiations. I don't want any further litigation pending."

"What you want and what my client wants are not necessarily the same thing," Mason said, "and under the circumstances I'm bound to do what I think is for the best interests of my client."

"That's what I'm telling you," Carson said. "The best interests of your client require that he cooperate with me and not go off half-cocked with a lot of litigation."

Mason said, "I want to ask you some questions, Carson, but I am going to ask you those questions when you are under oath and when you have an attorney representing you."

"Oh, I know," Carson said. "You've probably been talking with old squarehead Goodwin, the judge who tried the case. That old fossil! My gosh, you should see the way Vivian twisted him around her finger.

"After you've lived with a woman awhile, you get to know her pretty well. I could see the whole campaign, the way it was all thought out; the way she fluttered her eyes, the way she crossed and uncrossed her knees— looking at the old buzzard with her heart in her eyes— the perfect picture of the wronged woman. If Judge Goodwin could have done it, he'd have sent me to prison. Boy, did she sell *him* a bill of goods!"

Mason said, "I don't care to discuss the merits of the divorce action with you, Carson, but I believe that your wife named another woman."

"All right, what of it? They didn't prove anything, just a lot of inferences. Genevieve Honcutt Hyde is a friend, and that's all. Sure, Vivian had suspicions but she wasn't

32

able to prove anything. I spent a lot of time in Las Vegas but gambling was the main attraction. Sure, the girl was there and I liked her and I went out with her; a few dinners at nightclubs, automobile rides and stuff like that . . . Good Lord, the last few months of our marriage Vivian was like an iceberg to me. What the hell does she think a man's going to do? Work hard all day wrestling building problems, putting across deals, and then come home to some frosty-faced reception committee of one that starts finding fault before he's got the door closed?"

"I have told you repeatedly," Mason said, "that I don't care to discuss the case with you. And just so there won't be any misunderstanding, I suggest that you leave the office now. Use that exit door to the corridor."

Mason got to his feet.

"Okay," Carson said, "throw me out. I thought I could drop in and have a friendly little chat with you and perhaps Morley and I could get things all straightened out."

"If you want to talk with Morley Eden there's no law that prevents you from doing so," Mason said.

"Oh, to hell with both of you," Carson said, pushing his way toward the door. "You go your way and I'll go mine."

Carson pulled the door back with a jerk.

"Good morning, Mr. Carson," Mason said in a loud voice.

"And a good morning to you, *Mr.* Mason," Carson shouted. "I tried to cooperate with you and didn't get anywhere. Now, when you want to find me, you can hunt me up."

Carson swung his broad shoulders out through the door and pounded his way down the corridor.

Paul Drake, apparently on his way to the men's room, barely glanced at the irate figure.

"A delightful personality," Della Street said as the door closed. "Imagine being married to *that.*"

"He probably has his good points," Mason said thoughtfully, "but he likes to throw his weight around and when people aren't impressed he becomes rather objectionable.

33

When the initial fascination of marriage fades, two people can get on each other's nerves mighty fast."

"He's so darned assertive and domineering," Della Street said. "He—"

She broke off as a buzzer sounded.

"That probably means the typing department has the complaint ready in the case of Eden versus Carson."

Mason said, "When Morley Eden comes in to sign the verification, Della, see that it is notarized. I'm going to try and do one good turn."

"What?"

"I'm going to make whatever amends are possible to a woman who seems to have been caught in a cross fire."

"You mean Nadine Palmer?" she asked.

Mason nodded.

"She may not welcome you or any suggestions from you."

"She may not," Mason said, "but at least I'm going to tell her what the score is."

Mason looked at his watch. "As soon as this action is filed there'll be a furor of publicity. Tell Mr. Eden to answer all inquiries from reporters by stating that he will have open house for a press conference at one o'clock and photographers can take whatever pictures they want. Tell him I'll be at his place as near one as I can make it, and to wait for me. Tell him to be sure not to unlock the front door or to let anyone in until I arrive. Then he can give all the newspaper reporters a simultaneous story and I'll see that he doesn't give any wrong answers."

Della Street, her pencil flying over the page of her notebook, looked up and nodded.

"All right," Mason said, "I'll sign the complaint as attorney for the plaintiff. Right after Eden signs it and it's notarized, send it down to the courthouse and file it."

Della Street said, "May I make one secretarial observation?"

"Shoot, Della."

"You need a haircut, Chief. If you're going to have your picture taken at a press conference, and if you're

34

going calling on a good-looking divorcée, you should have—"

"Go no further," Mason said. "I'll go get my hair cut right now, and have a manicure to boot."

"*I* didn't mention the manicure," she said.

"I know," he told her. "That was my own idea."

Chapter Five

THE WOMAN who opened the door a scant half an inch in response to the chimes was unusually tall, graceful and gave the appearance of being completely self-reliant. She was holding a robe tightly across her chest.

"Yes?" she asked inquiringly, looking at Mason with frankly appraising eyes.

"I'm Perry Mason, the attorney," Mason said. "I—"

"Oh," she interrupted, "I knew I'd either seen you or seen your picture. This is a real pleasure, Mr. Mason. I'm Nadine Palmer— although I suppose you know or you wouldn't be calling. However, I'm simply not presentable. I was just out of the shower when I heard the chimes."

She hesitated a moment, then gave him her hand, extending it with a certain deliberation which made the gesture seem that she was extending to the lawyer a part of her personality.

"May I come in for just a moment?" Mason asked.

"I'm not presentable . . . oh, well, come on in. You'll have to wait for me to get some clothes on."

"Thank you," Mason said. "It's important or I wouldn't bother you."

Mason followed her into the small but tastefully furnished apartment.

She indicated a seat by a reading table and said, "What is it, Mr. Mason, am I in trouble?"

35

"Were you expecting trouble?" Mason asked.

She said, "I've had troubles and I will probably have more. Now if you'll excuse me I'll change."

Mason said, "Go right ahead. I'll wait although I haven't much time. I have to go to a press conference. I'm attorney for Morley Eden. Morley Eden, in case you didn't know, purchased some property from Loring Carson and . . ."

At the mention of Carson's name her eyes flashed, her mouth tightened. Halfway to the bedroom she paused, whirled to face him. "Just what do you have to do with Loring Carson?" she asked ominously.

"At the moment," Mason said, "I am not violating any confidence in telling you that I am about to file suit against him for something over three hundred and fifty thousand dollars in damages on the ground of fraud, asking for triple compensatory damages, and for exemplary damages."

"I hope you collect every last red cent," she said.

Mason smiled. "Evidently he is no great friend of yours."

"That louse!" she said, spitting the words out contemptuously. "He's torn my reputation to shreds and hung the tatters up before every gossip columnist in the city."

"I understood there was some mistake," Mason said, "and—"

"Mistake!' she snapped. "There wasn't any mistake. That man deliberately tried to blacken the name of his wife, and the fact that he dragged me down in the process made not one bit of difference to him."

"I believe your name *was* mentioned?" Mason asked.

"Mentioned?" she said. "He screamed it all over the city. He filed a cross-complaint stating that his wife was carrying on an affair with one Norbert Jennings, that they had made trips together over weekends, his wife registering under the fictitious name of Nadine Palmer.

"Then, after his wife stood by her guns and contested the suit, the heel had the audacity to state that it was all a mistake, that his private detective had shadowed the wrong person; that he had inadvertently pointed me

36

out to the detective instead of his wife, that his wife was not the person who had registered in various weekend resorts, but that it was I, one Nadine Palmer, a person whom his private detective had been shadowing under the misapprehension that the woman was his wife.

"You can imagine where that has left me."

Mason nodded sympathetically.

Abruptly she seated herself. "You're a lawyer, Mr. Mason. You've seen women in bathrobes before. You don't have much time and neither do I. Okay, let's talk it over and get it settled right now.

"People make me sick! There's more hypocrisy about our civilization and our so-called code of morals than anyone wants to admit. When I married Harvey Palmer, I was what is referred to generally as a 'good girl.' That was the trouble with me. I didn't know enough about men. I didn't know enough about life and I knew virtually nothing about sex.

"I went through five years of all the degrading hell to which a woman could be subjected, and then I decided that since there weren't any children I certainly owed Harvey Palmer nothing more. I walked out. Just to show you how dumb I was, I waived all claim to alimony. I had been a working girl before I was married and I went back to being a working girl—only I was no longer a girl. I was a woman.

"That's one thing about divorce, Mr. Mason, that the books don't tell you about. You've changed from a girl to a woman. You're on your own. You have found out that matrimony isn't all a bed of roses, yet you're a human being with normal appetites and desires and you're marked. You're indelibly marked.

"Any man who takes an interest in you is keenly conscious of the fact that you aren't a girl any longer, that you're a woman; that you've been married. He treats you accordingly. If you don't respond the way he thinks you should respond, you're 'holding out on him.'

"Men go around bragging about their conquests. Married men have mistresses. It's all taken as a part of life by society. But a divorcée is neither fish, flesh, fowl nor herring. She's supposed to be a pushover.

"And now comes this . . . this unspeakable cad, with his private eye. I can't tell whether the private eye was too dumb to know the difference or not, but this much I do know. Loring Carson was, is and always will be a heel.

"Norbert and I were very close friends. I think he was going to ask me to marry him and under those circumstances I probably would have said yes—but I wasn't going to walk into it with my eyes closed. I'd done that once. I wasn't going to do it again.

"Now Norbert feels he's been made ridiculous. He . . ."

"Has changed his mind about asking you to marry him?" Mason asked.

"Changed his mind?" she said. "Heavens, no! Now the man is insistent. He calls me up, proposing marriage two and three times a day. I hang up on him. And why is he doing all that, Mr. Mason? Simply because he feels that it was through him that what people refer to as a 'girl's good name' was besmirched.

"I'm over twenty-one, I'm divorced and I've got a right to live my own life. I just wish society would let me alone. And as far as Loring Carson is concerned I hope he drops dead . . ."

She threw back her head with a little toss, as though shaking unpleasantness from her mind, and said, "Now I've unburdened myself and spat out my venom, Mr. Mason, and perhaps after having been guilty of inflicting my personal spleen on you, I'll be polite enough to let *you* explain the purpose of *your* visit."

"It's quite all right," Mason said. "I came here to try and spare you some publicity."

"How?"

"This suit that I have filed against Loring Carson, or which is probably being filed at about this time, is rather spectacular. I don't know whether you're familiar with the real estate deal between Carson and Morley Eden."

She shook her head.

"Well," Mason said, "there were two adjoining lots. One of the lots was held to be the separate property of Mrs. Carson, one was community property which the court awarded to Loring Carson. It was purchased by

38

Morley Eden for a fair consideration and to which Morley Eden therefore had a good title—and that includes title to the portion of the building resting on that lot.

"Two persons had their reputations affected by Loring Carson's cross-complaint—you and Vivian Carson, his wife."

"I have every sympathy for her," Nadine Palmer declared.

"So, apparently, does Judge Goodwin," Mason said.

"What has he done about it? I understood Carson had his financial affairs so badly tangled up the court couldn't even begin to get them straightened out."

Mason said, "It's always a mistake to underestimate a judge's intelligence."

"Meaning that Carson underestimated Judge Goodwin's intelligence?"

"I think so."

"Would it be fair for me to ask you what is happening?"

"That's why I'm here," Mason said. "I felt you should know. Judge Goodwin feels that once a woman's good name has been sullied it is very, very difficult to get it unsullied."

"He can say that again!" Nadine said fervently.

"When a newspaper publishes a story," Mason went on, "it is given prominence in accordance with its reader interest. For instance, the story of a woman who has been stepping out and has been caught in the act rates considerable publicity. Later on, the fact that it was all a mistake rates no publicity at all."

"Are you talking about *my* case now?" she asked.

"In reverse," Mason said. "Judge Goodwin is thinking about Vivian Carson. He would like to have Carson's mistake publicized. So he has placed my client in such a position that we have to take action. I think Judge Goodwin was very shrewd in his reasoning, but I think he overlooked one thing."

"What's that?"

"The effect on you."

"And what about the effect on me?"

"The step I am taking," Mason said, "is going to result in the newspapers giving great publicity to the comedy of errors, to the fact that you were pointed out to Carson's detective in place of Vivian Carson."

"I think that was all done deliberately," she said.

"That's not the point," Mason said. "The point is that the whole thing is going to be rehashed at great length in the press."

She started to say something, then suddenly the full impact of the lawyer's words dawned on her. Her eyes widened. "You mean they're going to bring it all up again about the weekend trips?"

"Exactly."

"Oh, Lord," she moaned.

Mason said, "Therefore, I felt that you might care to make some plans in advance. If you want to meet the press, you might care to hand out a written statement so that you wouldn't be misquoted. If, on the other hand, you *don't* want to meet the press, this might be a good time for you to be hard to find."

She hesitated only a moment, said, "I'm going to be hard to find. When is all this going to break?"

"Probably within the next hour."

She got to her feet, said, "Look here, Mr. Mason, do you have any objection to being quoted?"

"What do you mean?"

"That you advised me to make myself hard to find."

Mason thought for a moment, shook his head. "I'm not in a position to advise you. You're not my client. I already have one client in the case. I'm simply trying to give you a friendly tip."

"All right. Will you remember that you gave me a friendly tip and told me to make myself scarce?"

"That was one of the alternatives I suggested might be wise."

"It's the alternative I want to take," she said. "You wait there just a moment. I'm going to crawl in a hole and pull the hole in after me. What's more, I'm going out with you. You can drive me downtown."

She hurried across the apartment, opened a door, and just before she slammed it shut behind her called over

40

her shoulder. "Wait there until I can get dressed and throw some things in a bag. I'm getting out of here."

The lawyer seated himself, consulted his wristwatch, frowned thoughtfully, reached for the cigarette case in his pocket and found that he was out of cigarettes. He waited another minute, then called through the door, "Are there any cigarettes in here, Mrs. Palmer?"

Her voice sounded startling clear through the thin door. "In my purse there's a pack. The purse is on the table."

The lawyer moved over to the open purse, noticed a pack of cigarettes, took one out, snapped his lighter into flame and suddenly paused as he realized the cigarette was limp with moisture.

Abruptly the door from the bedroom flew open. Nadine Palmer, trailing an almost transparent negligee through which could be seen her figure in the scantiest of lingerie, came hurrying into the room.

"I hope you found it all right," she said.

She grabbed up her purse, fumbled inside of it for a moment, then produced a pack of cigarettes and extended it to the lawyer.

Mason shifted his position.

"Now wait a minute, that's not fair," she said, laughing. "You're jockeying me between you and the light. I'm not dressed to be silhouetted right at the moment. I'm just trying to be hospitable. Here."

Mason took one of the cigarettes from the package she handed him, surreptitiously dropping the first cigarette into the side pocket of his coat.

"Thanks," he said.

"I should have put you on your honor to close your eyes," she said. "Now just be patient for a minute. I'm going to let you drive me to the nearest downtown bus stop."

She whirled and, making a feeble and somewhat futile attempt to grab the negligee around her, hurried back to the bedroom.

The lawyer again snapped his lighter into flame. The new cigarette which she had handed him caught instantly and burned slowly. Mason looked in the open purse.

41

The package of cigarettes in the purse seemed to be exactly the same as the package from which he had extracted the damp cigarette. Examining the pack, however, he found each cigarette was perfectly dry.

Puzzled, Mason withdrew the other cigarette from his side pocket, felt it with an exploring thumb and forefinger. That cigarette was definitely water-soaked.

Mason sat in thoughtful silence smoking the cigarette, from time to time watching the smoke eddying up from the smoldering tip.

Before the cigarette was entirely finished, Nadine Palmer, attired in a neat, well-tailored suit, was in the room carrying an overnight bag, her purse and a small suitcase.

"I'll let you do the honors with the suitcase," she said. "Do you have a car here?"

"I have a car."

"Then may I ride with you until I can get a bus?"

"Certainly," Mason said.

"Which way are you going?"

"I'm on my way to see my client, Morley Eden. He's the one who purchased the Loring Carson property and had Carson build the house."

"You're on your way out there now?" she asked, almost, it seemed, in dismay.

"Yes."

"I'll ride part way with you," she said. "I'll get off at the first through bus line we encounter."

"You don't want a cab to come here?"

"I want to leave here with you because I don't want to be traced," she said, "and when the reporters get on the track of a spicy story of this sort they are veritable demons. They can ask the most embarrassing questions."

"I take it," Mason said, "that the registration was not in the name of Mr. and Mrs. Norbert Jennings, but was in your own name, at least as far as you're concerned."

"The registrations were okay," she said, "but they were very definitely weekend trips, and just as I told you, Mr. Mason, I'm not a girl, I'm a woman. People have a tendency to draw their own conclusions when they're

42

dealing with a divorcée—and I'm a divorcée. Shall we go?"

Mason picked up the suitcase, led the way to the elevator, then out to his car. He saw Nadine Palmer give a hasty, apprehensive look over her shoulder as he held the car door open. She jumped in with a flash of graceful legs and a dazzling smile.

"Thank you very much, Mr. Mason," she said. "You're a help, a big help—perhaps more of a help than you realize at the moment."

"Well," Mason said somewhat awkwardly, "it occurred to me that Judge Goodwin was thinking entirely of Vivian Carson and I thought that someone should think of you because, after all, you're just as much of an innocent victim as Vivian Carson."

"Not in the judicial mind," she said. "After all, I did permit myself to become interested in Norbert Jennings. I did go on various weekend trips with him."

"Where?" Mason asked.

"All sorts of places. You'll be reading about it in the papers. I'm afraid I was—oh, damn it, 'indiscreet' sounds like such a prissy word. I will put it this way: I was uncareful. I naturally didn't expect that a detective would be following along behind, keeping notes on everything I did."

"Was it so terrible?" Mason asked.

"It could be made to appear that way. After a floor show in Las Vegas Norbert escorted me to my room. We had some drinks there and talked. I guess it was two-thirty in the morning when he left. And, of course, there was this sneaky detective parked around the corner with a notebook and a stopwatch, keeping track of the time—and, of course, drawing his own conclusions."

Mason started the car, drove slowly down the street. "Did you," he asked, "ever know a woman in Las Vegas, a hostess by the name of Genevieve Hyde?"

"Why?" she asked.

"She seems to have been the girl friend of Loring Carson," Mason said. "As such she might be of some importance. Did you know her—ever meet her personally?"

She frowned thoughtfully. "I don't think so. I saw

43

some of the hostesses, of course, and have talked with many of them without knowing their names. I've been to Las Vegas quite frequently."

"With Jennings?"

"I've made several trips with him—I've made other trips. I like Las Vegas. I like the glitter. I like the excitement. I . . . I'll be frank with you, Mr. Mason. I like to gamble."

"Have you ever been there just by yourself?"

"Never. I always go in a foursome or with perhaps some escort as in the case with Norbert Jennings and— well, gambling is a little expensive for a working girl. . . . If an escort wants to furnish me with chips, I . . ."

"You say you didn't ask for alimony?" Mason asked, as her voice trailed away. "May I inquire just how you do get along?"

She said hurriedly, "There's a taxicab right over by those apartments, Mr. Mason! If you'll let me out here, please, right here at the corner! I'll take a cab instead of a bus."

She lowered the car window. "Taxi," she called. "Taxi."

Mason eased the car to a stop. The cab driver nodded, opened the door of the cab and hurried over to pick up the baggage from the lawyer's car.

"Thank you *so* much, Mr. Mason," she said.

She blew him a saucy kiss, then turned to the cab driver.

Behind Mason a car honked its horn and the lawyer moved on into traffic.

Chapter Six

PERRY MASON drove up to the Eden side of the house, noting that half a dozen automobiles were filling every available parking space there. As he rolled smoothly to a stop in the middle of the driveway, a newspaper photographer with a camera and flashgun came running toward the car.

Other photographers, seeing the running cameraman, scurried into activity and soon Mason's car was surrounded with popping flash bulbs.

As Mason opened the car door, a reporter said, "What the hell? We've been out here nearly fifteen minutes! This guy says we can't get in the house until you arrive."

"I'm sorry if you were kept waiting," Mason said.

"You can't keep a newspaper waiting," the man said, "but the city editor wants an interview from you. Come on now, we're in a rush. Let's get the door open and and take a look. What the hell is this all about?"

"Have you tried to get in the other side of the house?" Mason asked.

"No one answers the doorbell and the door is locked. We've been around and got photographs of the exterior and all that, but the place is all locked up. I understand Mrs. Carson was a model, and Eden says she parades around in a very abbreviated bathing suit."

"I didn't say any such thing," Eden interrupted indignantly. "I said nothing about her *parading* around. I said that at one time she was taking a sunbath in an abbreviated bathing suit."

"It's all the same," the reporter said. "Come on, you've got a key to the joint, let's open it up."

Another reporter said, "My city editor wants an interview with Mason. How about telling us what it's all about, Mason?"

The lawyer said, "I'll give you a very brief summary of the facts in the case. I would prefer not to have my photograph taken. As an attorney I'm not courting newspaper publicity and—"

"Phooey," the reporter interrupted. "My editors want an interview and they want photographs. We've got photographs. Now come on, tell us what's it all about."

Mason briefly sketched the background of the litigation.

"And you filed this suit for fraud?" the reporter asked.

"That's right. We've asked for punitive or exemplary damages, as well as actual damages."

"And Carson told Eden that he had the deadwood on his wife, that he had a detective who had traced her to various weekend resorts where she'd been having a torrid affair with some guy. Is that right?"

"As to that," Mason said, "you can get your facts from Morley Eden, or from the pleadings. I prefer not to discuss that phase of the case, and naturally I would prefer not to have it tried in the press but in a courtroom."

"Lawyers have ideas about ethics and all that stuff," the reporter announced, "but newspapers exist for the purpose of getting news. This is a hell of an interesting situation. You may not want to talk about it, but the newspaper is going to make a whale of a yarn out of it. If you give us the facts we'll have them straight. If we have to get them from someone else we may have them garbled. You have any idea when Mrs. Carson is going to be back?"

Mason shook his head. "I didn't know she was away."

"We need a little cheesecake," the reporter said. "A photograph of her in that bikini suit on one side of the barbed-wire fence, and Morley Eden on the other, would be knockout. He says she handed him a cup of coffee early one morning. Maybe we could get her to pose handing a coffee cup through the barbed wire."

"I have nothing to say about Mrs. Carson," Mason said.

"Your client would go for it if we could fix it up?" the reporter asked.

Mason caught Eden's eye. "My client would *probably* go for it." he said.

"This is going to make a helluva story," one of the reporters said. "Any objection to us going in now and going through the place?"

"Only one side of it," Mason said. "Morley Eden's side."

"Well, it is his house. He had it built. Does he have keys to the other side?"

"He has keys to the other side, but there's a restraining order. He can't set so much as a foot on the property. He can't even put his hand or arm through the barbed-wire fence unless he has permission from the owner of the property on that side."

The reporter said. "Damn it, I'll bet my editor is going to make us wait here until we get cheesecake to go with the art work."

He turned to Morley Eden. "Haven't *you* any idea where Mrs. Carson is? Didn't you see her go out?"

"I got here just about the same time you did," Eden said. "If you remember, you drove in right behind me."

"And you haven't as yet been in the house?" Mason asked.

Eden shook his head. "Miss Street told me not to open up until you got here. I was afraid to unlock the door for fear they would push in past me. These fellows are in a hurry and they want a story."

"We're not in such a big hurry we aren't going to get the whole story." the reporter said. "Let's go inside. We want a picture of you standing on the springboard of the swimming pool in a bathing suit but afraid to dive for fear you'll come up on the other side of that barbed-wire fence. Haven't you *any* idea where Mrs. Carson is?"

Eden shook his head, took a key ring from his pocket and unlatched the front door.

"But you do have a key to the other side of the house?" the reporter asked.

"I have a key that did fit the side door. I haven't tried it since the restraining order was served on me. I don't know whether the locks were changed or not. I do know

47

they had a locksmith out here so they could get the door open. It may be he changed the locks."

Reporters and photographers moved in a compact group into the reception hallway. "Which way to the swimming pool?"

Eden pointed.

They started hurrying down the steps to the living room, then suddenly the leaders recoiled.

"Hey, what's this?" one of the men said.

"Someone's lying there!" Eden exclaimed.

"Someone's not only lying there," Mason said, "but there's a pool of blood. You boys had better keep back and . . ."

His words were wasted as reporters and photographers surged forward. Flashlight bulbs filled the room with spasmodic spurts of brilliant illumination.

Mason moved far enough forward so he could see the features of the man lying on the floor, then whirled and raced for a telephone. He found one in the hall.

"Operator," he said, "this is an emergency. Get me police headquarters."

When he had police headquarters he said, "Homicide, please . . . I want Lieutenant Tragg. Is he in?"

"Who is this talking?"

"Perry Mason."

"He's around some place, Mr. Mason. Just hang on. He . . . Here he is now. Hold on."

Mason heard the man's voice say, "Lieutenant Tragg, Perry Mason wants to talk with you." Then, after a moment, Tragg's dry voice came over the wire, "Now, Perry, don't tell me you've found a body."

"I haven't," Mason said, "the reporters have and they're trampling all over the place getting photographs."

"What place? What body? What reporters? Where are you talking from?" Tragg asked crisply.

Mason said, "It's a house that was put up by Loring Carson on property selected by Morley Eden. Morley Eden is here now and the man who is sprawled in the living room, and who apparently has been murdered, is Loring Carson. It's a difficult place to find, but my secretary, Della Street, has a map that will show you exactly how to get here and—"

"We've got maps here," Tragg said. "Give me the street and number. If there isn't a number on the street, give me the description from the tax record or the deed. Give me anything and keep those reporters away from that body."

"I stand as much chance keeping reporters away from that body as I would keeping a flock of moths away from a light," Mason said. "Here, I'll let you talk with Morley Eden. He'll tell you how to get here."

Mason nodded to Eden, who had moved up close to the attorney. "You tell him, Eden," Mason said. "It's Lieutenant Tragg of Homicide. I want him to get here before all the clues have been obliterated."

The lawyer handed the phone to Eden and ran back to the living room.

One of the reporters was kneeling beside the body.

"Look at those diamond cuff links," he said. "See what the guy has done. He's put some kind of black stuff over those diamonds so they don't glisten, but you can see where some of it came off. That's a diamond underneath all right and . . . Hey, you fellows, his shirt sleeves are all wet."

Mason bent down beside the reporter. "Homicide is on its way out here," he said. "They'd like to have the scene kept intact."

"Sure they would," the reporter said, "and my newspaper wants the news. Now as I understand it, this guy is Loring Carson. He's the divorced husband of the woman living on the other side of the fence; he's the man who built the house, the fellow who sold the lots to Morley Eden?"

"That's right."

"What's he doing here?"

"I don't know," Mason said. "How wet are the shirt sleeves?"

"They're good and wet, but the sleeves on the coat aren't wet."

"How did he die?" Mason asked. "I noticed blood. Was there a shot or—"

49

"Look around on this side and you can see how he died," the reporter said. "There's a wooden-handled butcher knife sticking into his back, and I mean it's sticking all the way in. Just the handle protrudes."

"*Both* shirt sleeves are wet?" Mason asked.

"That's right, *both* shirt sleeves, but the sleeves of the coat aren't wet."

"How high are the sleeves wet?"

"To the elbows. I'm not going to take the coat off or disturb the position of the body in any way. You can feel the wet cuffs and shirt sleeves."

Abruptly one of the newspaper reporters broke away from the group and sprinted for the hall.

As though his departure had been a signal which triggered action, there was a general scampering exodus.

One of the men grabbed Morley Eden. "A phone," he demanded. "Where's a phone?"

"There's one in the hall and—"

"That's being used."

"There's one in my bedroom."

"An extension or a main line?"

"A main line."

"Lead me to it."

"Hey, Mac," one of the others said, "you can't hog it. You can get first call but that's all."

"The hell I can't hog it. I'll stay on the line until I've got my story in and it's quite a story."

"Where's the next nearest phone?" one of the men asked Mason.

The lawyer shook his head. "There's a service station up where this road leaves the main highway. I don't know of any other place."

A few moments later the lawyer was left alone in the room with the sprawled figure of Loring Carson.

Mason surveyed the dead man, then moved slowly along the room.

Near the body, and at a point almost directly under the barbed-wire fence, the glint of reflected light caught Mason's eye. He bent down to examine the source of the light and found two little pools of water, perhaps no more than three teaspoons of water in each pool, and directly between them the mark of a foot where evidently one of the reporters had been standing in such a way that he caused the water from the edge of one of the little pools to spread into a muddy smear.

Hurriedly Mason moved to the door which opened onto the patio and looked across to the swimming pool.

There could be no question that there had been activity around the pool. There was still a puddle in a shaded section of the tiles on Morley Eden's side, and on the sunny side at the shallow end there were very definite indications of recent moisture.

Mason turned and hurried back into the house.

"Morley," he called. "Oh, Morley."

They met in the hall, Morley Eden emerging from the direction of the bedrooms.

"Any more phones in this house?" Mason asked.

"Not on this side. There's one in the other side."

"A main line?"

"A main line."

"You have a key that will fit that side of the house?"

"Sure I have a key. That is, it used to fit, but I don't dare use it. I—"

"Give it to me," Mason said.

Eden hesitated for a moment. "You know you could get in trouble with this and—"

"Give me the key," Mason told him. "Hurry!"

Eden took a leather key container from his pocket, selected a key and unsnapped it from the container. "This did fit the side door," he said. "I don't know whether it does now . . ."

Mason didn't wait to hear him but, grabbing the key, dashed out through the door, hesitated a moment as he surveyed the fence, then decided he could make better time rounding the fence in his car than by trying to run for it. He jumped in the car, switched on the ignition and sent gravel flying as he spun the wheels in taking off down the driveway.

When he came to the heavy post embedded in cement, the lawyer slammed on the brakes, whipped the car into a skidding turn around the end of the fence, dashed up the driveway on the other side of the house, stopped his

51

car directly in front of the side door, ran up the steps and fitted his key.

The key clicked back the lock.

Mason hurried into the house through the utility room, looking frantically for the telephone, found it in the kitchen, picked up the receiver and dialed the number of Paul Drake's office.

A few second later, when he heard Drake's voice on the line, Mason said, "Paul, this is Perry. Get this; get it right, get it fast and get started."

"Okay, go ahead."

"Nadine Palmer, a divorcée living at 1721 Crockley Avenue, left her apartment house with me about an hour ago, maybe a little longer. When we reached the main intersection—there's a row of apartments there called Nester Hill—she saw a cab standing at the place reserved for a two-cab stand on the right-hand curb. She took that cab and went somewhere. I want to find out where she went. When you find her, I want her tailed.

You're going to have to contact the cab company. You're going to have to find out what cab was there. You're going to have to find out where it went. You're going to have to pick up the trail of Nadine Palmer and do it fast. I want to know everywhere she goes. I want to know everyone she sees. I want to get the whole dope on her and I don't want her to know it, and I don't want anyone to—"

Mason turned abruptly as he heard an exclamation from behind him.

Vivian Carson, her arms full of grocery bags, stood in the doorway looking at him with indignation.

"Well," she said sarcastically, "make yourself right at home, Mr. Mason! If there's anything you want, just go ahead and take it."

"I'm sorry," Mason said, hanging up the phone, "I had to get to a telephone in a hurry."

"So it would seem," she said. "I heard your instructions, I presume it's all right to eavesdrop in one's own house."

Mason said, "I'm sorry."

"I'm afraid simply saying you're sorry isn't going to

52

be enough. I regard this as a deliberate violation of Judge Goodwin's order."

"That's all right," Mason told her. "I'll be responsible to Judge Goodwin. Now let me ask you where *you've* been."

"I've been shopping," she said.

"How long have you been gone?"

"None of your business."

"It may not be my business," Mason said, "but it's going to be the business of the police."

"What do you mean, the police?"

"I mean," Mason said, "that your ex-husband, Loring Carson, lies murdered just on the other side of that fence. Someone pushed a knife into his back and it just might be a good plan, Mrs. Carson, to find out whether—"

Vivian Carson's arms opened. First one bag of groceries, then the other crashed to the floor. A carton of milk spilled open, a bottle of salad dressing broke. Milk and salad dressing mingled together on the waxed tile floor.

"My husband . . . mur . . . murdered," she repeated, as though trying to accustom her mind to the words.

"That's right," Mason said, "murdered, and the police—"

He broke off as the sound of a siren screaming around the turn in the road died to a low-pitched growl.

"The police," Mason finished, "are here now. Are there any other groceries in your car?"

"Two full bags," she said.

"Permit me," Mason said. "I'll bring them in for you."

The lawyer detoured the mess of spilled groceries on the floor, said, "Perhaps you'd care to show me just where they are."

Vivian Carson started to follow him, then shook her head, braced herself against a wall for support, moved a few staggering steps to a chair and collapsed into the seat.

Mason went out to her car, noticing the squad car on the other side of the fence at the Morley Eden entrance.

The lawyer opened the car door, carefully looked in, found two shopping bags filled with groceries, took them

53

in his arms, carried them to the house, noticing, as he did so, that all of the police activity was centered at the other side of the residence. Apparently the officers had not seen him.

Mason brought the groceries into the house, paused before Vivian Carson.

"Where do you want these, Mrs. Carson? In the kitchen?"

"Yes," she said. "Please."

"Come on," Mason told her.

"I . . . I can't . . . I . . ."

"Nonsense," Mason told her. "Get up out of that chair and tell me where to put these groceries."

At the peremptory tone of his voice, she arose from the chair, took a few uncertain steps, then led the way slowly into the kitchen.

Mason dropped the groceries on a table, said, "Now look, Mrs. Carson, I want to be absolutely fair with you. While I'm in here, I'm going to look around."

"What do you mean?"

"Your husband was murdered," Mason said. "The police are on the other side of the house right now. The minute you open the door between the kitchen and dining area you'll see them in the living room on the other side of the fence. They're going to question you."

She nodded silently.

"Now then," Mason said, "you're a pretty poised young woman. You have been around. You know what it's all about. You hated your husband's guts. I don't know why you should be so shocked over his murder unless you had something to do with it."

"What do you mean?"

"Did you kill him?" Mason asked.

"Who, me? . . . Heavens, no!"

Mason nodded in the direction of a long magnetic bar which was just to the right of a big electric range. A dozen or more knives were suspended from this magnetized bar.

"It looks as if there might be a gap there," he said, pointing to a vacant space. "All of the other knives are arranged symmetrically and evenly spaced, then there's this gap and—"

"One knife is in the icebox," she explained. "I put it in there with some bread I had been slicing. Why this sudden attempt to pin a murder on me? Do you have some client you're trying to protect?"

"Let's put it this way. I'm giving you a dress rehearsal before the police start asking you questions. How long has this shopping trip of yours kept you away from the house here?"

"A couple of hours, I guess."

"Just getting groceries?"

"I stopped at the supermarket and got the vegetables on the road home."

"And where were you during the rest of the time?"

"Driving around and doing a little window-shopping."

"See anyone you knew?"

She shook her head.

"In other words," Mason said, "no alibi."

"What do you mean, no alibi? Why do *I* need an alibi?"

"Figure it out for yourself," Mason invited.

"But you said Loring was on the other side of the fence, in the other part of the house and . . ."

"His body," Mason said, "is lying within a few inches of the barbed-wire fence. He may very well have staggered a few steps before he fell. He could have stood on one side of the fence, you could have stood on the other, and you could have pushed that knife through the fence.

"There's one other possibility. You could have slipped into the pool, dived under the barbed wire, entered the living room, stabbed your husband and then returned the same way."

"All right, I *could* have! That doesn't mean I did."

"Where's your bathing suit?"

"It's a skimpy suit. I've been a model, Mr. Mason, and frankly I think a lot of our so-called modesty about our figures is the result of hypocrisy and unclean thinking. I'm proud of my figure. I guess I'm something of a nudist. I—"

55

"Never mind all that," Mason interrupted, "and never mind how skimpy your bathing suit is, *where* is it?"

"In the shower room off the pool—and it's wet. I took a late afternoon swim yesterday and washed out my suit. I intended to hang it out in the sun to dry today but realize now I forgot to do so."

"All right," Mason told her. "I'm glad to see I've snapped you out of it. Someday you'll thank me."

"What is it you're supposed to have snapped me out of?"

"Of the blue funk that was gripping you when you first realized you were going to be questioned by the officers. Now then, clean up that mess, get rid of the broken glass and all of the junk before the police get over here to question you. You've got your self-possession back, now keep it."

Mason ran quickly from the kitchen through the utility room to the side door, walked out and got in his car. No one noticed him as he drove down the graveled driveway to the big post set in cement and to which one end of the fence was anchored.

He left his car in the driveway, ran up the steps to the house, found the front door standing open and was about to enter when a uniformed officer in charge of the small group of newspaper photographers and reporters herded the group out of the door. "You boys know the rules as well as I do," the officer said. "We'll give you all the facts we feel we can release, but you can't go trooping around getting all the clues messed up and you know it. You had no business down there in the first place. Now you're going to have to wait outside until the inspection is over. We can arrange for you to use the phone, but that's all."

Mason walked through the reception hall to the arched doorway and looked down. One officer was roping off the section of the living room where Carson's body was lying. Another was questioning Morley Eden, who looked up and said, "Oh, *there* you are, Mason! What the devil! I've been looking all over for you. The officer wants to know who put in the call, who discovered the body, what you had to do with it and all of that stuff.

I told them they'd better ask you." He came up the steps.

"Quite right," a dry voice said from behind Mason's shoulder. "You *should* make an explanation, Perry."

Mason turned to face Lieutenant Tragg's enigmatic professional smile. "Another body?"

"Another body," Mason said.

"Getting to be quite a habit with you, isn't it?"

"It's also a habit with you, isn't it?" Mason asked.

"That's my business," Tragg said. "I come in contact with bodies."

"So do I," Mason told him. "I didn't discover this one. The reporters discovered it."

"And you happened to be here at the time?"

"I happened to be here at the time."

"How delightfully opportune," Tragg said. "Now perhaps you'd like to tell us about it, Mason."

Mason said, "I think you'd better take a look down there first, Lieutenant. The reporters have done a lot of trampling around."

Tragg frowned, looked down at the sprawled body and said, "The officers seem to have the case in hand now. I'll talk with you for a moment. What's the idea of the fence running through the house, Mason?"

"Judge Goodwin's idea," Mason said. "This house was involved in a divorce action. Judge Goodwin divided it."

"Who's living on this side?"

"Morley Eden, the gentleman standing there beside you."

"Your client?"

"My client."

Tragg said, "How do you do, Mr. Eden. Why did you think there was going to be a murder here?"

"I didn't," Eden said.

"Then why did you think you needed Perry Mason?"

"For your information," Mason said, "I have just finished filing a suit for fraud against Loring Carson on behalf of Mr. Eden. That is why the newspaper reporters were here."

"I see, I see. And who is Loring Carson?"

"The man who built the house; the man who sold the

57

lots; the defendant in the divorce action and the corpse down there on the floor."

"Well, well," Tragg said, "that seems to cover the situation pretty well. Now who's living on the other side of the house?"

"Acccording to Judge Goodwin's ruling, that belongs to Vivian Carson."

"Wife of the man down there?"

"She is now a widow," Mason said.

"I stand corrected," Tragg observed with a bow of mock humility. "And do you have any idea where Mrs. Carson is now, Mr. Mason?"

"I would assume she was over in her side of the house."

"And how do I get to the other side of the house?"

"There are two ways," Mason said. "You can dive from the springboard of the swimming pool and swim under the barbed-wire fence, or you can go around the heavy post at the end of the driveway where the fence starts, then go up the other side of the driveway and through the side door of the house."

"Or," Tragg said, pursing his lips, "you might crawl under the fence?"

"You *might* crawl under the fence," Mason conceded, "but it would be a rather hazardous occupation for a man of even average build. That's a five-strand barbed-wire fence. The wire is heavy-gauge, and it's stretched just as tight as human ingenuity and modern mechanical appliances can stretch it."

"A woman with a slender figure could very probably wriggle under that lower wire without too much difficulty, particularly if she were stripped down to—to what one might call the bare essentials, Mason. Eh?"

"Or in a bikini," Mason said. "Bear in mind that the thought is yours, Tragg. I didn't suggest it to you, I only clothed your suspect."

"Oh, not *my* suspect, Mason. Not *my* suspect," Tragg said. "I was merely surveying the possibilities—the *bare* possibilities."

Tragg, frowning thoughtfully, moved over to stand for

a brief moment in the center of the archway, surveying the living room.

One of the officers, catching his eye, called, "You'd better look over this way, Lieutenant. There's a significant wet spot here as though someone had spilled some water, perhaps out of a glass."

Tragg started to walk down the steps, paused, then, turning back to Mason, said, "I think a slender woman could have slipped under the fence; a woman wearing a bikini, a *wet* bikini. Thank you very much for the suggestion, Perry. I'll remember it."

"It wasn't my suggestion," Mason said. "It was your idea."

"Exactly," Tragg said, smiling, "it was *my* idea and *your* suggestion."

Chapter Seven

MASON TOOK Morley Eden's arm, escorted him back a few feet into the hall.

"How did Loring Carson get in this house, Eden?" Mason asked.

"I wish I knew," Eden said. "The only explanation I have is that when Carson built the house he must have had duplicate keys made so that he could get in and out while he was putting on the finishing touches.

"You see, he erected the house and hung the doors but there was still a lot of work to be done on the interior and, of course, contractors don't like to have the public trooping and out of a house."

"Carson didn't turn all the keys over to you when the house was completed?" Mason asked.

"I thought he did," Eden said somewhat irritably. "He turned over two complete sets of keys, but there must have been a third set which he retained."

"You had no idea he was going to be here in the house?"

"Of course not."

"Where were you?"

"I went to your office this morning to sign the verification to the complaint. You were out somewhere. I read the complaint and signed the verification. Miss Street acted as notary public. She said I was to meet you here at one o'clock and that I wasn't to let any reporters inside the house until you arrived."

"Then what did you do?"

"I went back to my office."

"And what happened after you reached your office?"

"There were lots of calls from newsmen asking about the suit you'd filed. I told everyone I would be at the house at one; that you'd be there then and that I'd give them a statement at that time and let them take photographs. I said that in the meantime I had nothing to say."

"You had no idea Carson's body was in the house?"

"Of course not."

"How long since you've seen him?"

"Some time."

Mason said, "Carson was in my office. He tried a lot of bluster, but as nearly as I could gather the main purpose of his visit was to try and keep me from filing any action on your behalf. He told me that he was engaged in some rather delicate negotiations and that having a lawsuit filed against him at this time would put him in a most embarrassing position."

Eden frowned. "I had an idea that he was negotiating some sort of a deal and wanted to avoid publicity until the deal was consummated."

"Any idea what sort of a deal it was?" Mason asked.

Eden shook his head.

Mason said, "The man had a breezy informality about him. I assume that was his natural manner. Knowing that I was about to file suit against him for fraud, I didn't want to discuss anything with him. I kept telling him to get an attorney. He told me he didn't need one, that he could talk with me, and chided me for being something of a stuffed shirt as far as legal ethics were

60

concerned. Frankly he made me feel just a little embarrassed. He had a friendly manner of wanting to talk and get things settled on a man-to-man basis, and I had to adopt the position that I couldn't discuss things with him unless his attorney was present."

Eden said, "That was Carson's way. He'd put on the pressure and keep putting on the pressure. When he wanted something, he just kept boring right in."

"How did he get out to the house here?" Mason asked. "Did he come by car?"

"I don't know. There was no car parked here when I arrived except a couple that the newspapermen came in. Then two more press cars followed just behind me."

Mason said, "One thing is certain, he didn't *walk* out here. He either came in a taxicab or someone brought him. If he had someone with him, that person could have driven his car away. Did you come right out here from your office?"

"Actually I didn't," Eden said. "A woman phoned me and said she had some information on a piece of property I wanted to buy. She said that if I'd meet her out there in half an hour she'd show me how I could save ten thousand dollars on the deal and if I did that she'd want one thousand dollars as her cut."

"What did you do?"

"Told her I'd meet her there and listen to what she had to say."

"Who was she?"

"Wouldn't give her name, said she was a stranger to me but that she'd be wearing a dark green outfit with a white carnation corsage."

"Dark green," Mason said musingly. "That's where the original mix-up between Vivian Carson and Nadine Palmer took place. They were both wearing dark green. All right, you went out there. Did you meet the woman?"

"No. I waited half an hour. She never did show up."

Mason frowned. "That delayed you?"

"You might say . . . although your secretary told me you had one person you had to see before you arrived and I didn't need to hurry—just so I got here at one."

"You didn't see anything of Mrs. Carson when you did get here?"

"No."

"Did you notice whether her car was there at her side of the house when you arrived?"

"No."

"Could it have been there without your noticing it?"

"Oh, sure. I had other things to think about. And it could have been in the garage. That's on her side of the fence."

Mason regarded him thoughtfully. "Let's get this time element straight, Eden," he said. "What time did you actually arrive here?"

"Heavens, I don't know," Eden said somewhat irritably. "It was a little before . . . well maybe a little after one. There's no use trying to cross-examine me."

"I'm not cross-examining you," Mason said. "I'm simply trying to get at the facts. I also want to know when you left your office. The police are going to want all this information pinpointed down to the last minute."

"Well, I can't give it to them," Eden snapped. "I can't run my business on a stopwatch basis. I don't know just what time I left where."

"You were alone?"

"Yes, I went out there to this corner lot I was negotiating for, waited around for this woman in green, then after half an hour or so I decided I couldn't wait any longer and so drove straight out here."

"Did you see the knife that was in Carson's body?"

"Yes."

"Have you ever seen it before?"

"I think I have."

"Where?"

"I think it's part of a set; that is, a duplicate of the set that Carson gave me."

"Carson gave you a set of knives?" Mason asked.

"That's right," Eden said. "He completed the house and I gave him his check in final payment and he said he wanted to make me a little present; that he'd put up a magnetic bar for knives by the range in the kitchen. He had a whole set there, starting from small paring knives

62

up to knives for slicing bread, knives for cutting roasts and a utility knife that had a wooden handle. I presume he got a set for himself at the same time. One of the knives in that set is very similar to the knife that was in Carson's body."

"But you don't know whether that knife came from the set he gave you or not?"

"Heavens, no, Mason. What are you trying to get at? I saw Carson's body lying there. I guess you saw it before I did. I tried my best to keep away from it. I went up close enough to make sure it was Carson. Then some of the reporters started questioning me. Actually I thought they had no business messing things up the way they were doing."

"They didn't," Mason said, "and don't become so annoyed with me for trying to get your story straightened out. The police are going to want to know everything about your movements. They'll want to know how much of your time can be accounted for. They'll ask you for the names of witnesses who can tell where you were."

"Well, I can't give them the names of witnesses. How long is all this going to cover—this period of time the police will want to know about?"

"That," Mason said, "will depend on what the autopsy surgeon finds as to the time of death."

"Well, they'll have to take my word for it," Eden said.

"They'll take your word for nothing," Mason said.

Mason stepped over to the archway leading to the living room where Tragg was down on the floor on his hands and knees, raising and lowering his head so as to get reflections of light from the moist spots on the floor.

"Will you want me anymore, Lieutenant?" Mason asked.

"Want you *anymore,*" Tragg repeated. "Don't be silly, I haven't started with you yet. And don't let Morley Eden go away. I haven't started with him."

"What are you doing now?" Mason asked.

"Right at the moment," Tragg said, "I'm trying to account for these spots of water on the tile floor. Now do you suppose by any chance these came from melted ice cubes?"

"Meaning that Carson had a drink in his hand at the time of his death?" Mason asked.

"Exactly," Tragg said.

"I wouldn't know," Mason said, "but I have a suggestion that you might care to consider."

"What's that?"

"As I have previously pointed out, it's comparatively easy to go from one side of the fence to the other by using the swimming pool. That is, the fence goes right along the surface of the swimming pool but doesn't go under water. A swimmer could dive under the fence and come up on the other side with the greatest of ease."

"You think this water may have come from the swimming pool?"

"There's a chance," Mason said. "Water in the swimming pool is, I believe, chlorinated more heavily than drinking water. If you had some small bottles and could get that water before it evaporates . . ."

Tragg turned to one of the officers. "When Mason gets this cooperative he has something in mind, a very definite something. I was about to suggest that we collect this water so we can make a chemical analysis and, of course, Mason, noticing that I was inspecting the puddles of water and anticipating what I had in mind, has now made a very constructive suggestion."

Tragg got to his feet, dusted off the knees of his trousers and the palms of his hands and said to one of the men, "Get on the radio to Headquarters. Tell the dispatcher to rush a car out here with some sterile vials and some small sterile pipettes. I want to get as much of this water as possible before it evaporates."

The officer nodded, hurried out to the police car to get on the radio telephone.

Tragg turned to Morley Eden. "Now," he said, "how did Carson get in the house? You don't leave the door open, do you?"

Eden shook his head.

"That is another thing I was about to comment on," Mason said.

"Go right ahead," Tragg said. "I've forgotten now who it was that said fear the Greeks when they were bearing

64

gifts, but as I remember it he took the gifts. I'll take all the verbal gifts you have to offer; but don't discount the fact that every suggestion you make increases my suspicions all the more."

"That's quite all right," Mason said, "just so we get the facts straight, then we can adjust them later."

"That, of course, is the big thing in a homicide. Get the evidence, preserve the facts. Now what were you going to suggest?"

Mason said, "I think you'll find that Loring Carson had a complete set of keys to this house. He built the house, you know, and then turned it over to Morley Eden. First he sold him the lots, then he went ahead and contracted to build the house on a basis of progress payments."

"I see," Tragg said. "Well, ordinarily we don't take anything from the body until after a representative of the coroner's office gets here, but in a situation of this kind time is of the greatest importance. I think we'll go through his pockets, men, and just make a list of the things we take out. We should have an official photographer here any minute and representatives of the coroner's office."

Tragg turned to Eden. "Could I trouble you for a sheet or a pillowcase, or something that we could put on the floor and into which we could put the things we take from the man's pockets?"

"I can get you a pillow slip right away."

"That will be fine," Tragg said.

He stood a few paces back from the body, surveying it with thought-troubled eyes.

"Something bothering you, Lieutenant?" Mason asked.

"A lot of things are bothering me," Tragg said. "Look at the man's shirt, a very expensive shirt, French cuffs; cuff links that are enameled black, but you can see that they are diamond cuff links. Some substance was put over the diamonds and then the whole thing was enameled black."

Eden appeared with a pillow slip. "Will one be all right, Lieutenant?"

"One will be fine, thank you," Tragg said.

He knelt by the body, then started removing articles from the pockets.

"Well, well," he said, as he opened a folded book of traveler's checks, "five thousand dollars in hundred-dollar traveler's checks in the name of A.B.L. Seymour. It looks as though our man had an alias for purposes of his own, perhaps fooling the income-tax department. Perhaps we'll find he has a little love nest somewhere with all the complications that go with a dual life.

"Now in this wallet," Tragg went on, "are thousand-dollar bills, fifteen of them. And here's a wallet in his hip pocket with hundred-dollar bills. This man was what you might call well heeled. Now let's see. You are interested in the keys . . . Here are the keys."

Tragg extracted a leather key container.

"Now, Mr. Eden, if you'll step down this way with your house key, I'll check it with the keys in this key container and see if perhaps Mr. Carson had, as you suggested, retained a key to your house. Pardon me, the suggestion didn't come from you, it came from Perry Mason. Not, of course, that it makes any great difference in one way, but in another way it makes all the difference in the world. I have found that suggestions made by Mr. Perry Mason are nearly always pertinent but quite frequently tend to confuse the issues rather than clarify them, at least for the moment."

Morley Eden produced his keys.

"Now, let's see," Tragg said, "this is the key . . . to what? The front door?"

"The front door."

"There seems to have been a key removed from your key container. There's a vacant space there. Would you know anything about that?"

Eden glanced uncomfortably at Perry Mason.

Tragg said, "Well! Flashing signals of distress to your attorney, eh? So this vacant spot in the key container may well become *quite* significant. Perhaps we'll look into that first, Mr. Eden, if you don't mind. And if your attorney doesn't mind."

"Not at all," Mason said. "I asked Mr. Eden for the key to the other side of the house, which he took rather hurriedly from the key container and handed to me. With that particular type of key container, it's easier to pull the little lever and take out the key clips one at a time than to remove the key from the clip itself."

"I see," Tragg said thoughtfully. "And this key that was removed and given to you, Mr. Mason, what door does that fit?"

"The door to the other side of the house; that is, the side door."

"The side that was awarded to Mrs. Carson?" Tragg asked.

"That's right."

"Perhaps if you'd be good enough to produce that key, Mason, I'll check that key also and see if Carson perchance had keys to both sides of the house."

Mason handed over the key.

"Thank you," Tragg said with exaggerated courtesy. "You'll pardon me for rambling along here, just sort of thinking out loud, but I'm wondering if perhaps you didn't walk into your own trap. When you suggested that Carson had keys to the house and therefore could get in at any time you overlooked the fact that I'd ask Morley Eden for his keys in order to make a comparison. Of course when he produced his keys, the vacant place in the key container became readily apparent and so you were called upon to produce the key to the other side of the house. However, never mind. I take it the other side of the house is unoccupied at the moment?"

"Mrs. Carson lives there," Eden said.

Tragg, his shrewd eyes making a quick comparison of the keys he had taken from the body of Loring Carson with the keys in Morley Eden's key container, said "And why would Mr. Mason want the key to Mrs. Carson's side of the house?"

"I don't know," Eden said.

"I didn't think you would," Tragg said. "Mason, in his more subtle moments, seldom confides what he has in mind to anyone, least of all to his clients. Doubtless he thought he could protect your interests in some way, but perhaps Mr. Mason will be good enough to explain."

"I wanted to take a quick look in that side of the house to see if the murderer might be there," Mason said.

"That was brave of you, Mason."

"Oh, I don't know," Mason said casually, "the murder was committed with a knife. After a murderer uses a knife, he's finished with his weapon. It isn't like a gun which shoots one bullet after another."

"Now that's logical, very logical indeed," Tragg said. "And perhaps you thought the murderer was a woman? It's nice to have you civilians usurping the prerogatives of the police, but rather embarrassing at times. You *do* have a way of contaminating evidence, you know. Now I think, Mr. Mason, if you have no objection, you and I will walk right over to the other side of the house and we'll just see what it was you wanted to inspect."

"I think you'll find Mrs. Carson there now," Mason said.

"Oh, you do," Tragg said. "I take it that that use of the word *now* indicates that she wasn't there when you first went over, Mason."

"That's right, she'd been shopping."

"Well, well, we keep getting more and more information," Tragg said. "I think we'll now go talk with Mrs. Carson before she has a chance to do any more thinking about the instructions Perry Mason doubtless gave her."

Tragg turned to one of the men. "Now look," he said, "I want to get this moisture up from the floor; every drop that we can save. When the squad car comes and delivers these sterile vials and pipettes, I want you men to use them carefully. First you uncork the vial. Then you take one of these pipettes and insert it in the pool of moisture and gently suck on the other end of the pipette. That draws the moisture up into the pipette. Don't let it come up far enough to touch the end of the pipette or mingle with the saliva. Then remove the pipette from the puddle, put the end in the vial and blow gently until you have expelled the contents. Keep doing that as often as is necessary until you get both puddles absorbed.

"And when the coroner's office gets here, explain that I'm very anxious indeed to get the exact time of death. I want to know just as much as we can about that—postmortem lividity, body temperature. Find out when food was last ingested, check the contents of stomach and the large intestine. In short, get me everything possible on the time of death. . . . And now if you're quite ready, Mr. Mason, I think we'll go over and call on Mrs. Carson. I'll let you perform the introductions and after that, I'll thank you to refrain from any interruption until I have asked a few questions about your activities. Now, how do we go?"

"We go out the front door, down the driveway and around the big post with the wires anchored to it," Mason said.

"We can't get out around the swimming pool?" Tragg asked.

"Not around that way. It's a very deep lot. The barbed-wire fence goes right across the patio, crosses the surface of the swimming pool, goes across the tiled sun deck on the other side, and then down the hill for at least a couple of hundred feet."

"When she put up a fence, she put up a good one," Tragg said.

"I have reason to believe the purpose of the fence was to subject Morley Eden to the greatest amount of annoyance possible," Mason said.

"Well, it seems to have been rather effective," Tragg said. "I can't imagine someone living in a house with a taut, heavy-gauge barbed-wire fence running right through the middle of it. . . . But come, Mason, we're delaying matters, and somehow I have an idea that any delay is playing right into your hands. What did you tell Mrs. Carson?"

"I told her her husband had been murdered."

"Did you indeed," Tragg said. "Now that's very unfortunate. You know, Mason, the police like to be the ones who make announcements of that sort, and then we can see from the expression of surprise, regret or otherwise, just how the person takes the news. Sometimes we get very valuable clues that way."

"I'm sorry," Mason said, "but I thought she should know."

"You took it upon yourself to be a committee of one to tell her?"

"No," Mason said, "I went in that side of the house just to see if the murderer might be hiding there and she came in and ... well, she caught me by surprise."

"By surprise, eh? What were you doing?"

"Just getting ready to look around. No, come to think of it, I believe I was using the phone."

"Using the telephone?" Tragg said. "Well now, *that's* interesting. Let's see. The newspaper reporters were here. Evidently they came out to cover the story of the action for fraud on the house that was divided by a barbed-wire fence.

"When they saw that body lying there, that was a news dividend which must have made them think they'd hit the jackpot. I presume there was a brief period of inspection while photographers were messing around, and then the reporters dashed for the telephones and tied up every available telephone in sight. So you wanted to get to a telephone for reasons of your own, and all of the accessible telephones were taken. . . . I wonder if Mrs. Carson heard any part of your conversation."

"You'll have to ask her," Mason said.

"I certainly will," Tragg said, his eyes twinkling. "Please don't let me overlook that point, Mason. If it should slip my mind, just nudge me and call it to my attention, will you? And now if you're quite ready, we'll go across and meet Mrs. Carson."

"May I ask if any of the keys on Carson's key ring fit the doors of the house?"

"I can't tell you about that until I've tried them carefully," Tragg said, "but several of them seem to be identical. I think Mr. Carson probably did retain keys to the place. However, we'll make a more thorough test of the keys a little later on. Right now, if you don't mind, Mason, I'd like very much to have you introduce me to Mrs. Carson."

Tragg cupped his hand under Mason's elbow, kept pace with him as they walked back up the stairs and out of the front door.

"We have to go all around that fence at the end?" Tragg asked.

"That's right," Mason said.

"Well, I think we can make better time in a car. Here's one blocking the driveway. Is that by any chance yours, Mason?"

"That's mine."

Tragg held open the car door.

The group of reporters held in one place by the officer surged forward insistently. "Lieutenant, when are we going to have a chance to interview you?" one of the men called.

"In just a short time," Tragg said reassuringly. "I'm going to ask you boys to be patient. You've already photographed the scene and telephoned in your stories. I'll let you have news just as soon as there's any news to give you—provided, of course, it doesn't interfere with apprehending the murderer."

"Any ideas?" one of the men asked.

"I don't think I care to be interviewed at the present time."

"Where are you taking Mason? What's the idea?"

Tragg said in a low voice, "Come on, Mason, get that motor going. Let's be moving along."

The lawyer started the motor.

Tragg waved his hand reassuringly to the newspaper reporters. "You'll have to wait there a few minutes, boys," he said. "We don't want to have you messing up the evidence."

They drove around the fence post up the other side of the divided driveway.

"That fence certainly makes it inconvenient, doesn't it?" Tragg said.

"Very."

"If there hadn't been a double driveway, one going to to the front door and one going to the side door, it would have been *very* annoying."

"I think it's quite annoying even the way it is," Mason volunteered.

"Yes, I dare say it is. Now, Mason, did you use this key to the side door?"

"I used it."

"Did you have permission from the owner?"

"I had permission from the owner. Morley Eden is the owner."

"Well now, that's subject to question. I believe there's a decree of some sort, you said?"

"An interlocutory judgment which is not a final disposition of the matter," Mason said, "and then, of course, there's always the right of appeal. I prefer to reach my own legal conclusions from all the facts."

"Hum-n," Tragg said, "a typical lawyer's answer."

Mason parked the car in front of the side door.

"There was, I believe, a restraining order?" Tragg asked.

"I violated the restraining order," Mason said, "there's no question about that. That, however, is a matter between Judge Goodwin and me."

"I see," Tragg said. "I'm just getting the facts straight. Now if you don't mind, Mason, we'll first try this key to the door just so I can check on your story. It's not that I doubt your word at all, but I may have to testify in court later on, and you have a most devastating type of cross-examination, you know."

Tragg, keeping up a running fire of conversation, tried the key in the door, clicked back the lock, opened the door, then pulled it shut and pressed his finger against the bell.

Chimes sounded on the inside of the house.

A few moments later the door was opened by Vivian Carson.

"Mrs. Carson," Mason said, "this is Lieutenant Tragg of Homicide. He would like to—"

Tragg interposed his shoulders between Mason and the woman.

"Would like to ask a few questions," Tragg finished with his most engaging smile. "I must warn you that anything you say may be held against you and you do not have to answer without benefit of counsel. But I can assure you, Mrs. Carson, we sympathize with you and we're going to make this just as painless as possible. Now

72

just where were you at the time the murder was committed?"

"I don't know," she said, looking him straight in the eye, "because I don't know just when the murder was committed."

"Quite right," Tragg said. "That's a *very* good answer. One might almost think it had been suggested by Perry Mason's coaching.

"If you don't mind," Tragg went on, "we'll just go through to your part of the living room. By the way, just how is the house divided?"

"The fence runs through the living room. Most of it is on my side of the fence due to the dining area," she said. "I have the utility room, the kitchen, the showers and dressing room for the pool and the servant's quarters. I've been living in the servant's quarters."

Tragg said. "You have the kitchen?"

"That's right."

"May we look in the kitchen, please?"

She started to lead the way, when suddenly Tragg stopped and inspected the waxed tiles of the entranceway.

"Now you'll forgive me," he said, "but there's a spot here which has much less gloss than the rest of the tile floor. The refraction of light is not nearly as great—has something been spilled here?"

"I came in with groceries," she said. "Mr. Mason told me of my husband's death and I dropped the groceries. They were heavy and the strength just seemed to drain out of my arms."

"I see, and what happened?"

"Milk and salad dressing," she said. "The milk carton came open and the bottle of salad dressing broke. I cleaned the mess up."

"I see. Now, where was Mason standing?"

"At the telephone."

"And what was he doing at the telephone?"

"He was phoning someone."

"And did you hear the conversation?"

"I heard part of it, perhaps just about all of it."

"What did he say?" Tragg asked. "I'm very much interested in why Mr. Mason found it so necessary to get to a telephone that he would violate the restraining order of a court of law. After all, you know, an attorney is an officer of the court and is supposed to uphold the dignity of the court. What did you hear him say?"

"He was evidently giving instructions to someone on the telephone. He wanted to have someone shadowed."

"Did you get the name of the person he wanted shadowed?"

"Nadine Palmer."

Tragg's notebook was whipped out and his ball-point pen hurried across the page. "Nadine Palmer," he said. "Now do you know who she is?"

"Nadine Palmer," Vivian Carson said, "is the woman my husband's detective shadowed and reported to have been caught in indiscretions."

"Well, well," Tragg said, "and Perry Mason was telephoning someone to have her shadowed."

"That's right. He said that he wanted her tailed I remember the expression quite clearly."

"Yes, yes, wanted her tailed. Now did he mention the name of the person he was talking to?"

"No, I don't think so."

"Perhaps the first name," Tragg said, ". . . perhaps Paul?"

"Yes, yes, that was it!" she exclaimed. "I remember now, he called him Paul. That was just as I came in the house."

"And then what happened?"

"Then I think Mr. Mason sensed my presence and looked around, and I was very sarcastic and told him to make himself right at home and help himself to anything he wanted."

"And that sarcasm, I take it, rolled off Mason like water off a duck's back. But what did he say—what did he do as far as the telephone was concerned?"

"He simply hung up and at that time he told me my husband had been murdered."

"And you dropped the groceries?"

"That's right."

"You picked them up?"

"Yes."

"And where did you put them?"

"In the kitchen."

"Well, if it's all right with you, we'll take a look in the kitchen," Tragg said. "And, by the way, where did you buy groceries?"

"At the supermarket."

"The one near the top of the hill?"

"No, that's a rather small market. I said the *super*-market."

"Oh yes, and where was that?"

"That's down in Hollywood."

"You have the ticket?"

"Oh yes, I have the ticket from the adding machine."

"That's fine," Tragg said. "Those tickets are usually numbered and we can find out a lot about the time you were there by checking the number on the ticket and checking with the records of the cash register. Now if you'll just lead the way, please."

Vivian Carson went into the kitchen.

Tragg's eye caught the groceries piled on the sink.

"*Four* bags of groceries," he said. "Four big bags."

"Yes."

"Now let's see," Tragg said, "since Mason was in the house when you arrived and since you dropped two bags of groceries, those must have been the *first* two bags. Then you returned and got the second two bags and . . . ?"

"Mr. Mason got the second two bags for me."

"Oh," Tragg said. "I should have realized Mason would be very considerate. And where were you while he was getting the groceries? Did you perhaps go to the living room or open the door a crack so you could peek in and see what was happening?"

"No. I simply collapsed. I sat in that chair until after Mr. Mason returned."

Tragg's eye roving around the kitchen caught the knife rack.

"Now here's an interesting situation," he said. "A knife rack with all sorts of knives attached to it by a magnetic bar—since the murder was committed with a knife . . . You'll pardon me, Mrs. Carson, if I make an inspection."

Tragg stepped over to the knife rack.

75

"You can see," she said, "that they're all there."

"I can, I can indeed," Tragg said. "At least they *seem* to be all here. All evenly spaced and . . . What's this?"

Tragg reached up and removed a wooden-handled butcher knife from the rack.

"Just one of the knives," she said.

"Well now, is it?" Tragg asked, turning it over in his hand thoughtfully. "It's a knife all right, but it seems to have been unused. It has a price in crayon written on the blade, three dollars and twenty cents."

She said, "I just moved in you know, Lieutenant. I've only been here a short time. I haven't had a chance to get fully provisioned and I—"

"But you've been here since—since when?"

"Since Sunday. I moved in Sunday. We put the fence in Saturday afternoon and I moved in Sunday morning."

"All this time and haven't had occasion to look at the knives," Tragg said. "By any chance, Mrs. Carson, while you were out shopping you didn't deliberately buy a knife that would replace the one that had been plunged into your husband, did you?"

Vivian Carson started to answer the question, then suddenly stopped and caught herself. "I . . . I . . ."

Mason interposed smoothly, "You don't *have* to answer Lieutenant Tragg's question, you know, Mrs. Carson."

Tragg turned to regard Mason with considerable displeasure. "And we don't have to have your company here, Mr. Mason," he said. "You've performed the introductions, you've served your purpose here. Now you just don't need to bother to hang around. Mrs. Carson and I are going to get along perfectly."

"I believe it is Mrs. Carson's house," Mason said. "I think she can decide who she wants to have present."

"That's not the way you were talking a moment ago," Tragg said. "You thought it was Morley Eden's house and, as I remember it, there's a restraining order preventing anyone from coming on these premises and as an officer of the law I might have to forcibly eject you, Mason. You wouldn't want to be put in the position of resisting an officer—and furthermore, I *could* take Mrs. Carson up to headquarters for questioning, you know.

76

"Now, just to keep matters from reaching an impasse, I'm asking you to go right back through that entranceway and out the side door. You can get in your car, drive back to Eden's part of the house and wait for me there. On your way, Counselor."

Mason bowed. "Because of the restraining order, and because Mrs. Carson knows she doesn't need to make any statement at this time, I will be only too glad to leave."

"And to wait at Eden's place until I get over there," Tragg reminded him.

"And to wait," Mason said, catching Vivian Carson's eye and frowning slightly as a warning to her.

Chapter Eight

IT WAS twenty minutes later when Tragg returned to Eden's side of the house. He found Mason and Eden in the living room.

"How was the interview with Mrs. Carson?" Mason asked.

"Not very satisfactory, thanks to you." Tragg said. "However, the lady told me quite a few things. She gave me more information than she realized."

"I see," Mason said. "Now how would you like me to give you some more?"

"I don't think I'd like it," Tragg said. "I fear you when you're bearing gifts, but go right ahead."

Mason said, "I would like to call your attention to the fact that Carson's shirt sleeves are wet up to the elbow, but the coat sleeves aren't wet except on the inside where water presumably soaked in from the shirt."

"And how do *you* know all this?" Tragg asked.

"I know," Mason said, "because a newspaper reporter told me so."

Tragg said, "You have very carefully called my attention to this thing. Just what do you think it means?"

Mason said, "There is a swimming pool on the place and we have a man whose shirt sleeves are wet up to the elbow. I think the two things go together."

"All right," Tragg said, "we'll look around."

Tragg started toward the swimming pool, then turned as he noticed that Mason and Eden had fallen in behind him.

"I don't think I'll need either of you to help me look, Counselor," he said.

"My client," Mason said, "will need me to keep track of what you find."

"Well, your client's wishes don't control me in the matter."

"All right then," Mason said, "I'll put it up to you this way. Do you have a search warrant?"

"I don't need one. There's been a murder committed and I can look around for evidence."

"That's quite right," Mason said, "and you have a right to keep all people away who may obscure or remove the evidence, but when you leave the vicinity of the murder and start prowling around the premises without a search warrant, the legal representative of the owner of the premises is entitled to—"

"All right, all right," Tragg conceded irritably, "I'm not going to argue with you. Come along, but don't interfere and don't try to remove or suppress any evidence."

Tragg walked out to the swimming pool, surveyed the barbed-wire fence stretched in a taut line across the surface of the pool and across the patio.

"That's quite a job," he said. "Quite an engineering job, also."

Mason nodded.

"You'd have to dive to get under that fence," Tragg said. "The wires are too tight and too close together for a person to crawl through. Well, let's look around."

Tragg took off his coat, rolled up his sleeve, got down on his hands and knees and started feeling his way along the side of the swimming pool, his right hand in the water, exploring every tile of the swimming pool to the depth of his elbow.

"Just what did you think would be here, Mason?" he asked.

"I don't know," Mason said. "I though it was significant that the man's arms were wet."

"Of course it's significant," Tragg said, continuing to grope his way around the pool.

Vivian Carson, standing in the doorway of her side of the patio, asked, "May I inquire just what it is you're looking for?"

"Evidence," Tragg said curtly.

Tragg completed his circuit of the swimming pool on that side of the barbed-wire fence. "Well," he said, "I guess there's nothing here. We'll try the other side— although I don't see what you're getting at, Mason.

"Would you mind placing a chair next to the barbed wire on your side, Mrs. Carson? I'll place a chair on this side . . . right on the tile border of the pool will be all right . . . Thank you very much. In that way I can make an inspection without going all the way around."

Eden brought out a straight-backed chair which he placed on his side of the fence. Mrs. Carson brought out a similar chair.

Climbing to one chair and then stepping over the taut wire to the other chair, Tragg let himself down on the other side of the fence and completed his inspection of the pool.

"I don't seem to find a thing," he said, his manner thoughtful.

Mason pointed to the cement steps leading up from the shallow end of the pool. "Did you feel all around those, Lieutenant?"

"I felt all around those steps."

"And in back of the steps? From here it looks to me as though the first cement step isn't right up against the swimming pool."

"Well, what about it?" Tragg asked.

"Under ordinary swimming-pool construction," Mason said, "I thought—"

"Okay, I get it," Tragg said impatiently.

79

The police lieutenant got down on his knees again, said, "I'll probably have worn out the knees on these pants by the time I get done with this thing. I . . . You're right, Mason! There's a crack between the upper step and the back of the swimming pool. I can get my fingers in it. But that doesn't mean anything."

"No?" Mason asked.

"Wait a minute. Wait a minute," Tragg said. "There's a ring here."

"What sort of a ring?"

"A metal ring and it's on a cord. I'm going to pull it, Mason, and . . ."

Tragg braced himself with his left hand, pulled with his right.

"This thing is moving," Tragg said. "It's on a cable. It . . . Well, what do you know, what do you know?"

Some ten feet back from the swimming pool a tile raised on a hinge, disclosing a square receptacle.

Tragg let go of the ring, jumped to his feet.

"So that's it," he said, "a concealed strongbox. Let's see what's in it."

"You stay here," Mason told Eden, then climbed up on the chair and over the wire fence to Mrs. Carson's side of the house. He hurried over to join Tragg. They looked down into a steel-lined recess that was nearly eighteen inches square and some two feet deep.

"Not a darn thing in it," Tragg said.

Vivian Carson, standing behind them looking down into the dark interior, asked, "What in the world is all this?"

Tragg looked up. "Suppose *you* tell us, Mrs. Carson." She shook her head. "It's all news to me."

Tragg's brows knitted thoughtfully.

"Carson built this house, Mason?" he asked.

"That's my understanding."

"And the swimming pool?"

"The whole house, swimming pool, patio and everything."

Vivian Carson said, "So that's it! That's where he was concealing his money."

"What money?" Tragg asked.

80

"He jockeyed things around so that it was impossible to get any kind of a property accounting out of him," she said breathlessly. "Judge Goodwin knew that my ex-husband had been concealing assets and he was trying to force him to disclose them. He examined him at great length about whether he had any savings accounts, any safety deposit boxes, anything that . . . *That's* what he was doing when he constructed this house; he made this secret safe and he put cash and securities in here."

Tragg looked at her thoughtfully. "You're jumping to a lot of conclusions just because there's an empty hole here."

"All right," she said crisply, "what are *your* conclusions, Lieutenant?"

Tragg grinned. "I collect evidence. We arrive at conclusions *after* we get the evidence. If we jumped to conclusions and then tried to get the evidence to support those conclusions, we'd be in trouble all the time."

Mason said, "I think Mrs. Carson is making a perfectly obvious inference, Lieutenant."

"I suppose so," Tragg said, "but I always get suspicious of people who jump to too many conclusions too fast, even if they are logical. Is this the first time you ever saw this receptacle here, Mrs. Carson?"

"Yes."

"First time you ever saw this tile hinged back?"

"Yes, I tell you. I never knew anything about it. How does it work? Is it from someplace in the swimming pool?"

"It's worked from a place in the swimming pool," Tragg said.

Tragg went back again and inspected the step in the swimming pool. "Well, Mason," he said, "I guess that does it. We've solved the mystery of the wet shirt sleeves. If Carson was high-grading his income and kept things concealed from his wife, and probably from the income-tax people, this could have been his hiding place. Back of that cement step is a ring on a wire cable. By pulling it about two inches you actuate a lever and a spring raises this tile—and, of course, that furnishes a good motive for his murder."

81

"I'm afraid I don't understand what you mean by that," Vivian said.

"It's very simple," Tragg explained. "Loring Carson *may* have had a lot of money here—a great deal more than was found on his body. His wet shirt sleeves indicate he may have hurriedly opened the place of concealment and removed this large sum of money. Someone who wanted that money stabbed him and took the loot. It's that simple."

Mason said, "Who's jumping to conclusions now, Tragg?"

"I am," Tragg said. "I'm doing it because I wanted to see Mrs. Carson's reactions."

"All right," Vivian Carson said, "you can see my reactions right now. All you want.

"I'm trying to be fair, and I don't want to be a hypocrite. I'm not going to pretend a whole lot of grief that I don't feel. Loring Carson was a louse, a heel, but he was a human being and we had been married, which means, of course, that we had been very close. I'm sorry he's dead, but if property rights are involved I want to be protected. Anything that was in that place of concealment was really my property."

"How do you figure that out?" Tragg asked, looking up at her thoughtfully.

"Because Judge Goodwin wanted to award me more property. He felt certain that a substantial part of the community property had been concealed. Mr. Mason can tell you that. It's no secret. The judge said so in open court."

"Feeling that way," Lieutenant Tragg said, "if you had found out about this receptacle, you would have taken possession of any property that was in it?"

"Now just a minute," Mason said, "that's hardly a fair question. If she didn't know about the receptacle, she—"

"It's my question and it's a fair question," Tragg said. "It's a police question. Now I'm asking you, Mrs. Carson, if you had known about the receptacle, would you have taken anything that was in it?"

She met his eyes and said, "I'm not going to lie and I'm not going to be a hypocrite. I think I would have."

"Well," Tragg said, "at least you're frank and truthful. Under the circumstances, Mrs. Carson, I am afraid you're going to have to go with me to answer some more questions, and I'll be equally frank with you; we're going to get a search warrant for this house and we're going through it piece by piece. We're going to try to find what was in that receptacle."

"You mean I'm to consider myself under arrest?"

"Certainly not," Tragg said. "You can consider yourself as a young woman who is anxious to cooperate with the police in every way possible, who is only too glad to come downtown with me so you can answer questions and clear yourself of any possible suspicion . . . And, Mr. Mason, I'm going to ask the same thing of your client. I'm going to ask him to get in the car and go with us, and I may as well tell you, Counselor, that I'm going to ask you to leave the place at once. I'm going to get everybody out of here. I'm going to seal it up and then we're coming out here and we're going to search every nook and cranny."

"Go right ahead," Mason said irritably. "That's typical police psychology. You lock the door *after* the horse has been stolen.

"Loring Carson didn't walk out here. He came out here in a car. He probably drove his own car. Whoever came out here with him, took his car and drove away leaving him here. That means that in all human probability, Carson was dead when that other person left the house and—"

"I know, I know, I know," Tragg interrupted. "You're like all of these good citizens who want to tell the police how to run their business. For your information, Mr. Mason, very shortly after my arrival and as soon as I positively identified the corpse, I had the police put out an all-points bulletin for his car. We'll pick it up no matter where it is. We have the description of the make and model of the car and the license number.

"For your further information, we're watching the airport and making a check on the thruways. Whoever drives Loring Carson's car anywhere is going to be stopped, is

83

going to have to answer questions, and is, in all probability, going to be the number-one suspect.

"In the meantime, much as I value your suggestions, Counselor, I think the police can investigate this case without you. In view of this discovery, which changes the whole complexion of the case, I am now escorting you to the door. You're getting out and you're going to stay out. Mrs. Carson here and Morley Eden are going to ride downtown in my car; you have your own car here. I know you have a number of very pressing matters to which you must give your attention, and I am not going to detain you any longer . . . We're starting now—and I don't want anyone to touch that tile. I'm going to have the fingerprint men go to work on it—so just keep away from it, if you will.

"We're going now. I'll leave instructions with my men as we go out."

Chapter Nine

MASON FITTED his latchkey to the spring lock on the corridor door marked "PERRY MASON—PRIVATE," entered his office and encountered Della Street's startled eyes.

"You must have run into quite a mess out there," she said.

"I did," Mason admitted. "Do you know what happened?"

"Loring Carson was murdered, and at the moment I know very little else. What do you know?"

Mason said, "I know that the sleeves of his shirt were wet. His coat sleeves weren't wet, indicating that he had had his arms immersed up to the elbow while his coat was off; that he had put his coat on afterward.

"Lieutenant Tragg, following up that clue, found a cunningly concealed ring back of the cement steps lead-

84

ing down to the shallow part of the swimming pool. By pulling on that ring, one of the patio tiles swung back on a hinge, disclosing a steel receptacle that was approximately eighteen inches square and two feet deep. There's every indication that this was used as a concealment for valuables, but no one can prove it.

"Now then, Della, I want to get the time element straight. It seems to me that our client, Morley Eden, became rather vague about it. I'd like to fix the time of the murder as nearly as we can and I'd like to check up on a few other things.

"What time was it that Loring Carson came to the office?"

"I'll find out by consulting my daybook," Della Street said, "and can tell you exactly."

She crossed over to her secretarial desk, took out her daybook, said, "He was here a little after nine thirty-five. I've got a plus mark by the time. And he left here shortly before nine forty-five."

"Paul Drake was in the corridor and got a good look at him," Mason said. "Now then—and by the way, what about Paul? Has he made any report on that job I phoned in about?"

"He just told me he was working on it and told me that Loring Carson had been murdered."

Mason said, "See if you can get Paul on the line. Now let me see, I finished dictating that complaint in the fraud case about nine o'clock, didn't I?"

"A little before that, I think. You put the complaint on the dictating machine and I know that I had the typists come early this morning and they started typing a little before eight-thirty. The complaint was all typed before you went out, which was at about five minutes to ten . . . Did you get your hair trimmed?"

"I got the works," Mason said. "I got my hair trimmed, had a shave, a massage, a manicure and a shine. You told me that I needed to look my best for newspaper photographers and I thought it was a good idea."

"Or did you think that you needed to look your best for this Nadine Palmer?"

"Nadine Palmer," Mason said, "had something on her

mind. Della, suppose you were going swimming with nothing but your underthings on. What would happen?"

"Me?" she asked.

"You."

She said, *"My* underthings are in the mode and somewhat negligible. They are nylon and not designed for concealment when wet. I trust the question is scientific and impersonal."

Mason frowned. "It's scientific and impersonal and puzzling."

Della Street, whose fingers had been dialing the telephone as she talked, said, "Is Paul there? . . . Mr. Mason is in his office and he'd like very much to see him if he could step down for a minute.

"Okay, thanks," she said into the telephone, hung up and said, "Paul will be down here right away."

Mason took the cigarette from his side coat pocket.

"What's that?" Della asked.

"That," Mason, said, *"was* a very damp cigarette. Now then, Della, let us suppose that a young woman went swimming in panties and bra and then divested herself of her wet garments but didn't want to leave them where they would subsequently be found. She'd naturally put them in her purse, wouldn't she?"

"Unless she decided to wear them and let them dry while they were on her."

"I'm inclined to think Nadine Palmer squeezed the surplus water out of her undergarments and pushed them into her purse," Mason said.

"And why the swim in the near nude?" Della Street inquired.

"That," Mason said, "is something that may concern us very deeply. She——"

He broke off as Paul Drake's code knock sounded on the door.

Della opened the door.

"Anything on Nadine Palmer?" Mason asked as Drake stepped inside the office.

"Not a thing," Drake said.

Della Street said demurely, "There seems to have been *very* little on Nadine Palmer."

"How come?" Drake asked.

"It's just a theory I had," Mason said. "What did you do about the taxicab, Paul?"

"Oh, I found the taxi all right," Drake said. "She had the driver take her to the airport; but what happened when she got to the airport is anybody's guess. She may have taken a plane or she may have simply switched taxicabs and taken another cab back to town.

"If she took a plane, she didn't take it under her own name. My office has been telephoning every major airline trying to find a booking for Nadine Palmer and getting no place.

"I can tell you something else about your girl, and that is the police are looking for her."

"They are?"

"That's right. They have been making inquiries and told the landlady at the apartment house not to let anyone in the apartment until they could get a search warrant. They sealed up the apartment tight as a drum."

"Now that's something," Mason said. "Why would they do that?"

"I don't know, but they're working on a lead. The only thing is that they didn't know, or at least didn't seem to know, where she took the taxicab so we're one jump ahead of them on that."

Mason's eyes narrowed thoughtfully. "I said something to her," he said, "that touched off a whole chain reaction. I wonder what it was."

"What's this about her having nothing on?" Drake asked.

Mason said, "It was just a theory I had from a damp cigarette. Here's the cigarette, Paul."

"And how did you think the cigarette got wet?" Paul asked. "Being dunked in a swimming pool?"

"No," Mason said, "I had an idea Nadine slipped off her outer garments and went swimming in her undies. Then she took off the undies and squeezed what water she could from them, put them in her purse, got into her dress, and went home. And something I said to her rang a bell somewhere in her mind. I remember I was talking about Loring Carson and . . . Hey, wait a minute, I asked her . . .

"Della, start playing tunes on the telephone. Get me on the first available flight to Las Vegas. I'll call you when I get to the airport to find what one. I'll grab a taxicab and get out there just as fast as I can so I won't have any problem with parking. I should call you by the time you've got a confirmed reservation.

"Paul, stay on the job. Find out everything you can about Nadine Palmer. See if you can consult the records and find out what sort of an affidavit the police made in order to get a search warrant for her apartment.

"Della, the police are holding Morley Eden for questioning and they also have Vivian Carson. I don't think they'll hold either of them very long. As soon as they're released, Eden will probably call the office. Get him to come in. Tell him I'm concerned about the time element in the case. Get him to talk about everything connected with the time element; where he went; what he did.

"Make notes in shorthand, but don't be too obvious about it. I don't want him to get the idea we're putting him on the grid and applying pressure. The police have probably been all over it with him and his recollection should be fairly fresh at the moment.

"I'm on my way."

"I could drive you out," Drake said, "and—"

"I'll grab a cab," Mason told him. "You keep on the job here."

Mason jerked the door open, dashed out into the hall and sprinted for the elevator.

Chapter Ten

THE LAS VEGAS bellboy regarded the three one-dollar bills which Mason dropped into the palm of his hand and said, "Genevieve . . . sure, Genevieve is one of the hostesses."

"How about pointing her out?" Mason asked.

"Right this way."

The boy led the way down past a bar into a huge casino, where roulette wheels, wheels of fortune and rolling dice furnished a background of sound. Jacketed young women in tight-fitting slacks sat behind tables dealing twenty-one. At the far end of the room a bank of slot machines, whirring away busily, kept a continual monotone of sound interspersed occasionally by a voice over the loudspeaker announcing, "A jackpot on machine number twenty-one . . . jackpot on machine twenty-one . . . Machine fourteen hits the double jackpot. Machine fourteen hits the *double* jackpot."

The bellboy said, "There she is over there."

"Which one?" Mason asked.

"The snaky one."

"They all look snaky to me," Mason said.

The bellboy grinned. "They're paid to look snaky. She's the snakiest. The one on the right."

"Thanks," Mason said.

Mason walked through the milling crowd of sightseers and gambling customers to the far end of the room.

The young woman who had her back toward him was wearing a glittering, dark gown which fitted her like the skin on an onion. She turned as Mason approached, surveyed him with large, dark eyes that looked him over with a trace of impudence in their depths.

The gown followed the line of cleavage between her

swelling breasts in a low-cut V that started wide then narrowed until it seemed to stretch almost to her waist.

"Hello," Mason said.

"Hello," she said.

"I'm looking for Genevieve."

"You've found her."

"My name is Mason."

"Don't tell me the first name is Perry?"

"It's Perry."

"I thought I'd seen your picture somewhere. Now what in the world brings you to Las Vegas?"

"I'm looking for amusement."

"You're standing in the exact geometrical center of some of the best amusement in the world. Only don't make any mistake about me, I'm a shill, sucker bait, window dressing. I'm not for sale."

"Or rent," Mason said casually.

She smiled. "One might consider a long-term lease," she said, her large dark eyes looking up to the lawyer's rugged features and making no attempt to veil their interest.

Mason said, "I want to talk. Are you permitted to talk during working hours?"

"That's my business. I could lead you to a gambling table and . . ."

"My attention might become engrossed in other things," Mason said. "Could we have a drink?"

"That is not encouraged," she said, "except as a preliminary, but under the circumstances I think it might be done."

"In a booth?" Mason asked.

"In a booth," she said, "but there again remember that I'm on duty and in circulation. I'm supposed to lead customers to the gambling tables, to see that everyone is happy and once in a while to take a stack of chips and show the gamblers how easy it is to win."

"Is it easy to win?" Mason asked.

"If you know how," she said.

"And how does one learn how?"

"Come on, I'll show you."

She took Mason's arm, led him over to the roulette table.

"Give the man twenty dollars for a stack of chips."

Mason handed over twenty dollars and received a stack of chips.

"Now then, I'll make a bet with your money," she said. "You get the winnings."

She watched the wheel for a moment, then put chips on the number seven.

The wheel stopped on number nine.

"That easy?" Mason asked.

"Hush," she said, "I'm getting the feel of the thing. Put a couple of chips on twenty-seven and put some on double-zero. Put five chips on the red and three chips on the third twelve."

"At this rate," Mason said, "twenty dollars will last fast."

"And then," she said, in a half whisper, "I'll be free to go to a booth with you. They'll know I'm cultivating a customer."

The ball clicked into a pocket.

"See," she said.

Mason watched the croupier push out the chips.

"Now," she said, "you have a lot more than when you started."

Mason gravely handed her half of the winnings. "Could I make you a free-will offering?" he asked.

She accepted only a part of the chips, made quick bets around the board, leaned against him as she reached for the far end of the table so that Mason could feel her breast pressed against his left arm. Her lips were close to his ear. "I'm not allowed to cash chips," she said, "but cash is always acceptable later on after you've cashed in."

Mason said, "This is all rather new to me, Genevieve."

"When you're winning," she said, "press your luck. When you're cold, quit."

"That's the only recipe for success?"

"That's all there is to it. The trouble is the customer can't do it. When he gets cold, he starts trying to force his luck. When he's hot, he tends to get a little conservative. You're hot; shoot the works."

91

Mason watched her spread chips around the board.

Twice more the croupier handed out large piles of winnings.

Following Genevieve's lead, Mason started scattering chips in various places around the table and from time to time more chips were pushed across toward him.

People who were wandering aimlessly around came to watch the phenomenal success of the pair at the table. Soon the table was ringed with players so that spectators were crowded back into the second row. The play became so heavy that it took the croupier some time in between rolls of the wheel to rake in the chips, pay off the winners.

For a while Mason seemed to hit almost every third roll of the wheel, then there were five consecutive rolls during which he won nothing.

Abruptly the lawyer crammed the remaining chips into the pockets of his coat.

"Come on," he said to Genevieve, "I want a recess. I want to have a drink, I'm thirsty."

"You can have a drink served right here," she said so the croupier could hear her.

"I want to sit down and drink leisurely. Can I pay for it with these chips?"

"Oh, sure," she said, "or you can cash the chips in at the cashier's window and come back and buy another stack."

Mason followed her over to the cashier's window, handed in the chips, which were carefully counted, and received in return five hundred and eighty dollars.

The lawyer took Genevieve's arm, surreptitiously pressed a one-hundred-dollar bill into her palm, said, "Is that acceptable?"

"That's quite acceptable," she said without looking at the amount of the bill.

She led him past the bar over to a section of booths, slid in behind a table, smiled at the lawyer with full, red lips parted to show pearly teeth.

"You're a gambler," she said.

"I am now," Mason told her. "I've been initiated. Is it always that easy?"

"It is when you're hot."

"And what happens when you're cold?"

"When you're cold," she said, "you get mad. You start plunging. You get to feeling the board owes you money. Then you look at me with a jaundiced eye and think maybe I'm a hoodoo. About that time I slip one of the other girls the wink and she sidles over to the table, gets interested and makes a bet, leans up against you so she's pressing her form against you, says, 'Pardon me,' and smiles. You say something to her, and I'm sort of pushed into the background. Then if you don't do something to recapture me, I drift away and you have another hostess on your hands."

"And she collects a tip?"

"Don't be silly," she said. "No one who is losing gives anyone a tip, but when a man is winning he gets generous.

"My gosh, I've even seen 'em tip the croupiers down in a joint in Mexico until their pockets were bulging."

"Can the croupier control what happens?" Mason asked.

"How you talk," she said, laughing.

"I was talking about down in Mexico," Mason said.

"I know you were," she said, smiling at him invitingly.

A waiter paused by the table.

Mason raised his eyebrows inquiringly and Genevieve said, "Scotch and soda please, Bert."

Mason said, "Gin and tonic, double, please."

Genevieve adjusted her dress beneath the table, lowered her eyes, then suddenly raised them with an expression of surprise. "That was a hundred dollars you gave me," she said.

"Right," Mason told her.

"Well . . . bless your soul," she said, "and thanks."

"I may as well tell you that I want something," Mason said.

"All men want something," she said, smiling. "I hope what you want is something I can give. Something easily accessible."

She moved seductively toward him, then laughed and said, "Oh, let's forget it. Come down to earth. What do you want, Perry Mason?"

He said, "I want to know whether you know a Nadine Palmer."

"Palmer, Palmer, Nadine Palmer," she said, squinting her eyes thoughtfully and frowning slightly with an effort of recollection.

Slowly she shook her head. "The name means nothing to me," she said. "I might recognize her if I saw her. I know lots of people that are faces without names. Does she live here?"

"She lives in Los Angeles."

Again Genevieve shook her head.

"Do you know Loring Carson?" Mason asked.

Her eyes snapped up to his with hard appraisal, the pearly teeth vanished from behind the red lips.

"I know Loring Carson," she said.

"Have you seen him lately?"

She frowned. "It depends on what you mean by lately. I saw him . . . Well, let's see. He was here last week . . . I think it's been about a week since I've seen him."

"He's dead," Mason said.

"He's . . . he's *what!*"

"He's dead," Mason said. "He was murdered today, late this morning or early this afternoon."

"Loring Carson dead?"

"That's right. Murdered."

"Who killed him?"

"I don't know."

She lowered her eyes. For some ten seconds her face remained expressionless, then she sighed, raised her eyes to Mason and said, "All right, he's dead. He's gone."

"He was a friend?" Mason asked.

"He was a—a good guy; let's put it that way."

"You knew he was having trouble with his wife?"

"Virtually all men have trouble with their wives sooner or later. All the men that I meet do."

"He gambled quite a bit?" Mason asked.

"We don't discuss the affairs of customers publicly, but he gambled quite a bit."

"And won?"

"He was a good gambler."

"And that means what?"

94

"Doing just what I told you. There's no secret about it. Plunge like the devil when you're hot, lay off gambling when you're cold. Do that and you'll win, at least in Las Vegas. But people can't do that."

"Why not?"

"I don't know," she said.

"Carson wasn't like that?"

"Carson was a good gambler and when he was cold, he . . . he'd do what you're doing."

"What?"

"Take me out of circulation and buy me drinks."

"The management permits that?"

"Look, Mr. Mason, let's be frank. You're grown-up and I'm grown-up. You're a big boy and I'm a big girl. The management doesn't make much profit on the sale of drinks. The management puts out food, entertainment and lodging as cheap as possible.

"On the other hand, the State of Nevada is largely supported by taxes levied on the profits of gambling establishments. All this glitter and luxury is supported by one thing: the gamblers who don't know how to gamble, the gamblers who lose."

"There are gamblers who win?" Mason asked.

"There are gamblers who win."

"Consistently?"

"Consistently."

"And, I take it, what you're leading up to is that when a gambler is active and patronizes the tables, the management has no objection if you take a little time out to be with him."

"Under *those* circumstances," she said, "the management loves it. Now then, Mr. Mason, you're too smart a man to go back and start plunging and lose very much money. You and I will go back. If you're cold, you and I are going to part company. If you're hot, I'll be with you for a while. Something seems to tell me you're not going to be hot. I think you've made your pass at Lady Luck."

"And you think Lady Luck is going to turn a cold shoulder on me?"

"Lady Luck is a woman," she said. "Lady Luck is intensely feminine. You gave Lady Luck an opportunity to

95

smile at you and she did more than smile. She jumped in your lap. You indicated that you were gambling with only half of your mind on what you were doing. You were thinking of me. You were more interested in me than you were in Lady Luck.

"All right, you've had your tête-à-tête with me. When you go back to the table, something seems to tell me Lady Luck is going to be cold as ice."

"And if that happens?"

"If that happens, I'll drift to the perimeter and vanish. You'll find yourself with another hostess, provided you're gambling enough to be important enough to attract a hostess. If you're not, if you show signs of quitting when you're cold, you'll probably find yourself wandering around with no one taking very much interest in you."

"Interesting, isn't it?" Mason said.

"Business," she said. "Now what do you want?"

"I want to know if Nadine Palmer gets in touch with you," Mason said. "Nadine is a very personable young woman, well put together. I have every reason to believe she flew over here this afternoon from Los Angeles and I think she's looking for you. If she gets in touch with you, I'd like to know what it is she wants."

The waiter brought their drinks. Mason clicked glasses with Genevieve. "Here's how," he said.

"I know some cute answers to that," she said, "but somehow I think they'd be wasted and ... Look, Perry, I am going to be frank with you. That news about Loring Carson was quite a jolt to me."

"Were you fond of him?"

She hesitated a moment, then raised her eyes deliberately to Mason.

"Yes."

"Intimately so?"

"Yes.'

"Let me ask you this: Would you have become the second Mrs. Carson?"

"No."

"May I ask why?"

"I have my work, he has his. I'm a wonderful playmate. I'd probably make a damn poor wife. He was a

96

showman. He could treat a girl swell. I think he'd be lousy to a wife.

"Some men are like that. They're essentially salesmen. They like to sell their stuff and feel that they're getting an order on the dotted line, but when they've bought the merchandise, when it's in the house with them all the time, when it's eating with them, sleeping with them, traveling with them, they don't have any incentive to sell. And when they can't strut their stuff selling, they get bored. After they get bored, they get unresponsive. A man who's unresponsive is a net loss to himself and to the world."

"You don't seem to have a very high idea of marriage," Mason said.

"It's all right," she said, "for some people."

"Carson wasn't the type?"

"I don't think Carson would ever have been happy with any one woman until after he passed . . . oh, probably fifty, and by that time it would have been too late."

"For marriage?"

"For me. He'd have married some younger woman, someone in her twenties or someone in her early thirties who persuaded him she was in her late twenties."

"And then?"

"Then Carson would have wanted to settle down. He'd have felt that he'd hit the jackpot. The woman would have seen Loring getting old and slowing down. She wouldn't want to get old and slow down."

"And so?" Mason asked.

She shrugged her shoulders, finished her drink.

Mason tilted his glass, said, "Let's go back to the tables. Will you let me know if Nadine Palmer gets in touch with you?"

"For how much?"

"For two hundred dollars," Mason said.

"I'll think it over. It depends on what she wants. Is it something I could make money out of?"

"I don't know."

"I'm not going to lie to you, Mr. Mason," she said. "I hate liars. I've given up a lot of things coming over here to Las Vegas and being a hostess, but I've gained

97

certain things. One of them is the right to be free, and the right to be free gives me the right to be frank. Thank God, I don't have to lie anymore and I'm not going to do it."

"You used to lie?" Mason asked.

"Any girl who tries to be respectable, and isn't, has to put up a front."

She laughed. "You want lots of information for your hundred-dollar tip, Perry Mason. I told you I don't have to lie anymore. Come on, let's go back to the table. Let's see how hot you are."

She led the way back to the same table.

"Give the man a hundred dollars for chips," she said to Mason.

Mason passed out a hundred dollars.

The lawyer started putting bets around on the various numbers. This time Genevieve didn't help him, but simply stood there watching.

Time after time the wheel rolled and Mason collected nothing. He won a small bet on red and one on the second twelve, but the numbers eluded him and his pile of chips started shrinking.

Genevieve looked at him and smiled.

A young woman in a skin-tight dress abruptly reached a bare arm across the table, leaned forward to place a bet on a number at the extreme far corner. She stumbled slightly and her soft, pliant form pressed against Mason's arm.

"Oh, I *beg* your pardon," she said, and looked up and smiled.

"Quite all right," Mason said.

"Clumsy of me," she said, "but I just had a hunch on that number . . . Oh, oh, I didn't make it after all."

"Better luck next time," Mason said.

Her eyes met his. "There's always a next time," she said. "Always something new, always tomorrow—and today—tonight," she said softly.

She placed another bet at the corner of the board so that she pressed against Mason. This time she held the lawyer's arm.

"Pull for me," she said. "Wish me luck."

"You might give *me* some luck," Mason said.

"All right, we'll give each other luck."

The young woman's bet paid off.

"Goody, goody, goody," she said in an ecstasy of excitement, squeezing the lawyer's arm to her breast and jumping up and down. "Oh, goody, goody, goody, I made it!"

Mason's smile was enigmatic.

The lawyer made three more bets, which finished his pile of chips.

He backed away from the table.

"Oh, you're not quitting," the young woman said in a tone of incredulity.

"Just for a while," Mason said. "I'm taking a breather. I'll be back."

"Do," she said, and then added, "please." Then by way of explanation as though to apologize for any seeming attempt at being forward, "I had good luck with you here. You're so . . . Well, you brought me luck."

She looked wistfully after him as Mason drifted away from the table.

Genevieve Honcutt Hyde was nowhere in sight.

The lawyer went back to the bar, ordered another gin and tonic, sat there sipping and watching.

Fifteen minutes later, he saw Nadine Palmer moving through the crowd.

Mason pushed his glass away, followed Nadine to one of the tables.

Nadine was carrying a purse which was literally bulging with chips. She had evidently been drinking.

She pushed up to a roulette table and started making bets. Her luck was phenomenal. Within few minutes she had a crowd of people watching her play, trying to ride along on her bets.

Mason felt eyes on his and looked up to see Genevieve Hyde appraising him from the line of spectators.

He looked pointedly at Nadine, then back to Genevieve. Genevieve's face had no expression whatever.

Mason stayed in the background watching Nadine until finally Nadine had such a pile of chips in front of her, she seemed to be behind a barricade.

Then Mason leaned forward to put a lone dollar bill on number eleven.

"Cash in and check out," he said in a low voice to Nadine.

She whirled indignantly, then gasped with surprise.

"Cash in and check out," Mason said again.

The lawyer made two more bets, then stepped back from the table.

"You heard me," he said to Nadine.

Five minutes later Nadine, with two bellboys carrying chips, went to the cashier's window.

People watched her with awed curiosity as she cashed in something over ten thousand dollars.

Perry Mason took her arm as she left the window.

"*What* are you doing here?" she asked.

"And what are *you* doing here?" Mason asked.

"I'm gambling."

"You were gambling," Mason said. "You're quitting."

"What do you mean I'm quitting? I come over here every so often. I'm perfectly able to run my own life, Mr. Perry Mason, without any advice from you."

"The advice you're getting from me is purely gratuitous," Mason said. "I'm talking to you not as a lawyer but as a friend."

"You've become an intimate friend on rather short notice, it seems."

"I want to ask you some questions," Mason said. "Would you like a drink?"

"No, I've had enough to drink. I'm going out to my room. You want to come?"

"Is it all right?" Mason asked.

"What do you want me to do, hire a chaperon?'" she asked. "Or a baby-sitter?'

"Neither," Mason said, "I just wondered if it was all right."

She moved out of the side entrance, down the long line of bungalows, the lawyer at her side.

She fitted a key to a door, let Mason open it and then usher her inside. It was a sumptuous room with a bed, television, several deep easy chairs, wall-to-wall carpeting and an atmosphere of quiet luxury.

When Mason had closed the door, Nadine Palmer seated herself, crossed her knees, showing a generous display of nylon, surveyed Mason appraisingly and said, "This had *better* be good."

"It is good," Mason said.

"For your information," she went on, "I was hotter than a firecracker when you stopped me."

"How much had you won?"

"Plenty."

"I gathered you cashed in for around ten or twelve thousand."

"That was the second time I'd cashed in," she said.

"As much as that the first time?"

"More."

"What time did you get here?"

"I took a taxi to the airport," she said, "and took the first plane."

"You didn't buy a ticket under your own name."

"Is that a crime?"

"It might be taken into consideration in connection with a crime," Mason told her, "unless, of course, you had a good reason."

"I had a good reason."

Watching her, Mason said, "I have the distinct impression that you're simply sparring for time."

She said, "And I have the distinct impression that you're simply fishing for information."

"I'm not denying it," Mason said. "I'm asking for information. Why didn't you buy a ticket under your own name?"

"Because," she flared, "I'm tired of being an easy mark for every wolf in the world. Thanks to Loring Carson, my name has become a brand. I'm little Miss Pushover."

"Bosh and nonsense!" Mason said. "A few people read about what had happened in the newspapers, smiled a little, then turned the page and forgot the whole thing— at least, as far as you're concerned. I will admit that the situation is somewhat different as far as Vivian Carson is concerned. Loring Carson threw a lot of mud at her and I can see where she has been damaged."

"Well, save a little sympathy for me while you're at it,"

she said. "Every man I've met since that publicity has made passes."

"And didn't they make passes before that?" Mason asked.

"Look," she said, "I was having a winning streak. You came along with that big-shot, imperative manner of yours and told me I was quitting. You bluffed me into quitting. Now speak your piece, and then I'm going back to the tables. If you don't speak fast I'm going back anyway."

She got to her feet, smoothed her dress down and moved toward the door.

"Did you," Mason asked, "know that Loring Carson had been murdered when you left Los Angeles?"

She stopped midstride as he threw the question at her, and whirled, her eyes becoming large, her jaw sagging.

"Murdered!" she said after a tense moment.

"That's right," Mason told her.

"Oh, my God," she said. She walked back to the chair in which she had been sitting and dropped into it as though her knees had lost all their strength. Her eyes, wide and dark with expression, searched the lawyer's face.

"When?" she asked.

"I don't think they know the exact time; probably sometime late this morning or early in the afternoon."

"Where?"

"Out at the house he had built for Morley Eden."

"Who . . . Who did it?"

"They don't know," Mason said. "The body was found against the barbed-wire fence on the Eden side of the house.'"

"How was he killed?'

"He was stabbed with a butcher knife that may have been taken from the knife rack in the Vivian Carson side of the house. What makes it interesting is that there is some evidence indicating he had removed a large sum of cash from a place of concealment by the swimming pool, and the person who murdered him had taken that cash."

She sat looking at him, her manner indicating either

102

that she was having trouble getting the full import of his disclosure or that she was mentally dazed.

Mason said, "I may not have very much time to talk with you, Nadine, because the police are making a frantic effort to find you."

"The police! Why should they want *me?*"

"Because," Mason said, "there is some evidence indicating that the person who committed the murder picked up the knife on one side of the house, then got to the other side through the barbed-wire fence by means of the swimming pool.

"You'll remember that when I got to your apartment I found you with your hair wet. You were in a negligee. You said you had been taking a shower. Wasn't that rather an unusual time of day for you to be taking a shower?"

"Not for me it wasn't. What are you getting at?"

"And," Mason said, "I asked you for a cigarette. You told me to look in your purse. I looked in there and found a package of cigarettes. I took out one. It was soaked. I couldn't get it to light.

"You came dashing out of the bedroom, trailing your negligee behind you, careless of how much you were exposing because you were in such frantic haste to get at that purse. You grabbed it, whirled around, pretended to take the pack of cigarettes from the purse and handed it to me.

"Those cigarettes were quite dry. I think you had them in your hand when you came out of the bedroom."

"Indeed," she said sarcastically, "and what does all this mean, Mr. Sherlock Holmes?"

"It means," Mason said, "that you wanted to get from one side of the house to the other; that you stripped off your dress and dove in, clothed only in panties, bra and stockings; that afterward you swam back, squeezed the water out of your undergarments, put them in the purse, put on your dress, went home, and were just changing when I rang the bell."

"Meaning that I killed Loring Carson?" she asked.

"Meaning," Mason said, "that the police are going to regard all of these things as highly suspicious circumstances. Now then, when you got in the car with me I mentioned something about Loring Carson's girl friend, Genevieve Hyde, who is a hostess over here in Las Vegas. The minute you heard that name you suddenly got the idea you wanted to get out of my car and into a taxicab.

"I thought at the time it was because I had let a cat out of the bag; that you didn't know the name of Carson's girl friend and as soon as you found it out you decided you wanted to see her.

"Now I have another idea."

"And what's your other idea?" she asked.

"Now," Mason said, "I have a feeling that you may have suddenly acquired a bunch of cash; that you were wondering how to account for all that cash being in your possession, and when I mentioned Las Vegas it gave you a great idea. You decided you'd come over here, be seen plunging at first one gambling table and then another, and then later on you could say that you had been a heavy winner."

"Indeed!" she said. "But it happens that I *was* a heavy winner. You were standing there long enough to see that. You saw the chips I cashed in."

"Exactly," Mason said. "The fact that you came over here with the idea of camouflaging your sudden acquisition of wealth doesn't mean that you couldn't have run into a winning streak."

She looked at him speculatively for a few minutes.

"Well?" Mason asked.

"You're the one who's all wet, Mr. Perry Mason," she said. "I don't know anything about a wet pack of cigarettes. I didn't slip off my dress and go swimming in my underthings. I come over here to Las Vegas every so often in order to gamble. I love to gamble. Sometimes I'm very, very good at it. Usually I like to have a gentleman friend with me but I will admit that when you mentioned Las Vegas it rang a bell in my mind and I suddenly had the feeling that I was hotter than a stove lid; that if I could get over here I'd run right into a big winning streak.

"When I have a hunch like that I play it. Sometimes it's something that someone says that gives me a hunch

104

on a horse running in a race; then I dash out and make a bet on that horse. I like to play my hunches."

"And this was a hunch?"

"This was a hunch."

"Rather a rapid reaction," Mason commented.

"All of my reactions are rapid," Nadine said. "Where in the world did Loring Carson have all of this stuff hidden at the Eden residence?"

"It was an ingenious hiding place," Mason said. "He had evidently built it purposely while he was building the house. By pulling on a ring that was cleverly concealed behind the cement steps in the swimming pool, a hinged tile was elevated and that disclosed a steel-lined receptacle.

"When I left the place the police were planning to test the edge of this tile and the inside of the receptacle for fingerprints."

Despite herself, the expression on her face altered.

"Fingerprints!"

"Fingerprints," Mason repeated.

"You wouldn't . . . wouldn't leave fingerprints on a smooth surface like that?"

"On the contrary," Mason said, "the tape that cushioned the inside lip of the hinged tile would be an excellent place to leave fingerprints and it is very, very possible that the smooth surface on the interior of the steel-lined receptacle would take and hold a fingerprint."

"Mr. Mason," she said, "I . . . I want to tell you something."

"Now wait a minute," Mason warned, "I'm here trying to get information. I'm a lawyer but you're not my client. I have a client. If you tell me anything I can't keep it in confidence."

"You mean you'll have to tell the police?"

"Yes."

"Then I'm not going to tell you anything," she said abruptly.

"All right, don't," Mason told her. "But remember this: If—and mind you, I say 'if'—there should be anything that would be damaging to you in the evidence that the police are going to uncover, you don't have to make any statements to them.

"If you were out there, if you picked up that money or any part of it, the best thing for you to do is to see a lawyer of your own choosing."

She was silent for several seconds.

"Well?" Mason asked.

She said, "I was out there."

"At the pool?"

"No. I wasn't at the house at all. I had driven my car up to the point above the house. There are some lots up there that are for sale. I had been out there before and I saw that one could see this house, the patio and the swimming pool from that point."

"What were you doing out there? Now, don't answer unless you want the police to know."

"The police know—at least they're going to know.'"

"How does that happen?"

"A watchman for the subdivision caught me out there."

"Tell him you were thinking of buying a lot?"

"I couldn't. He caught me peeping with binoculars. I knew Norbert Jennings was going out there again with blood in his eye, looking for Loring Carson. He had a tip Carson was to be there. As the maligned woman who was to be the subject of a fight, I wanted to see the fight. Instead of that I saw . . ."

Abruptly her voice trailed into silence.

"Saw what?" Mason asked.

"I saw . . . saw . . ."

She ceased talking as the chimes sounded.

"That'll be the masseuse," she said parenthetically. "I left word for her to come here and . . ."

She crossed to the door, opened it and said, "Come on in. You'll have to wait for just a few minutes, I—"

She broke off and gasped as she saw Lieutenant Tragg's smiling face.

"Quite all right, thank you," Lieutenant Tragg said. "I'll come in, and if you'll permit me to introduce myself, I'm Lieutenant Tragg of Homicide of Los Angeles, and the gentleman with me is Sergeant Camp; Sergeant Elias Camp, of the Las Vegas police."

The two men moved into the room.

Tragg smiled at Mason and said, "You know, Mason, you're quite a bird dog, really quite a bird dog."

"You followed me here?" Mason asked.

"Oh, we did better than that," Tragg said. "We knew that you wanted to find Nadine Palmer and had had a detective trailing her, so we simply rang up the various airlines and asked if they had booked a Perry Mason any time during the afternoon for any destination.

"Now, Mrs. Palmer, here, didn't use her own name evidently, because we couldn't find where *she'd* taken a plane. But we found *you* had taken a plane here, and you're rather a distinctive individual, Mr. Mason. You stand out, you really do. You left quite a broad trail once you arrived here. We had little difficulty picking up that trail.

"We'd have been here sooner only we wanted to get a few formalities disposed of first."

Lieutenant Tragg turned to Nadine Palmer. "Now, Mrs. Palmer, you have been doing a little gambling since you arrived?"

"Yes. Is there anything wrong with that?"

"Not a thing. And I understand you've been rather fortunate?"

"Very fortunate, indeed—and I take it *that's* not illegal."

"On the contrary, that's very nice," Tragg said. "The Internal Revenue Service will be very interested. They always like to get an unexpected windfall of this sort. And where did you leave your winnings, Mrs. Palmer?"

"I . . . I have them here."

"That's fine," Lieutenant Tragg said. "Now this paper that I'm handing you is a search warrant, giving us authority to search your baggage."

"No!" she cried. "You can't do that! You can't . . ."

"Oh, but we can," Tragg said, "and we're going to. Now this handbag or purse here. It's lying on the bed as though you've put something in it in a hurry. Let's just see what we have here, if you don't mind."

Tragg opened the bag.

"Well, well, well," he said.

"That's money I won!" she cried. "I won it here gambling in Las Vegas."

Tragg stood looking at her, his smile deceptively cordial but his eyes hard as diamonds.

"Congratulations," he said.

Mason said, "I assume there's no further need for me to be here. You can remember what I told you, Mrs. Palmer, and . . ."

"Don't go, don't go," Tragg said. "I want you here for two reasons: First, I want you to hear what Mrs. Palmer has to say because you'll be a disinterested witness since you have other clients in the case, and second, I want to search you before you go."

"Search *me?*" Mason asked.

"Exactly," Tragg said. "Who knows but what you came here to present a claim on behalf of your client and received something in the way of a cash settlement. I'm quite sure we won't find anything, Mason, but it's a formality that the Las Vegas police insisted on. If you'll just stand there, please."

"Do you have a warrant to search me?" Mason asked.

The Las Vegas officer said, "We can take you down to the station, book you on disorderly conduct, occupying a room for immoral purposes, resisting an officer and a few other charges. Then we'll turn you inside out when we get you down there. You can have it whichever way you want. Now hold your arms out from your sides."

Mason smilingly held his arms out from his sides. "Go right ahead, *gentlemen,*" he invited.

"He's clean," Tragg said, "clean as a hound's tooth. I know him like a book. He'd have pulled some sort of a razzle-dazzle if he'd had anything on him."

The Las Vegas officer rapidly went through Perry Mason's pockets. "I guess the stuff is all there," he said, indicating Nadine Palmer's handbag.

"And quite a haul," Tragg said. "Several thousand dollars. Now, did you win *all* of this money at the tables, Mrs. Palmer?"

Nadine Palmer said, "I don't like your attitude, I don't like the way you come into my room and make yourselves at home, I don't have to answer *any* of your questions.

108

You're trying to browbeat me and intimidate me and I'm going to insist on having a lawyer of my own choosing here before I answer any questions."

"Is Mr. Mason the lawyer you have reference to?"

"He is not," she said, "Mr. Mason is representing the other people in the case. I want an attorney who will represent me and me alone."

Tragg stepped over, held the door open and bowed smilingly to Mason. "That, Counselor," he said, "is the cue for your exit. You've been searched, you have a clean bill of health, you aren't this woman's attorney. We're taking her to Headquarters for interrogation and we certainly don't want to detain *you*.

"I even understand that *you* were a little lucky at the gaming tables a while back. If you don't mind accepting a word of advice from a seasoned officer, I would suggest that now you've made your little pile of winnings, you stay away from the tables for the rest of the evening. They have an excellent floor show here, I understand.

"And of course you won't mind having the Las Vegas police keep an eye on you, Mason. We want to know where you go, what you do and with whom you talk. I wouldn't tell you this, only I know that you'll spot the gentleman waiting around the entrance to the casino as a plainclothes officer who has been instructed to keep you in sight. In such cases if there's a mutual understanding it's always so much easier all around."

Tragg bowed with mock deference as he held the door open.

Mason turned to Nadine Palmer, "I think you've made a wise decision," he said. "Get an attorney."

"Are you presuming to advise her?" Tragg asked.

"Just as a friend, not as an attorney," Mason said.

Tragg said to Nadine Palmer, "Mr. Mason is representing other people in this case. Everything he does is done for *their* best interests. Quite naturally if he can get *you* involved with the police, it's going to make things a lot easier for his clients. I'm just telling you this so you can take everything into consideration. I wouldn't want you to labor under any misapprehensions, and I'm quite certain Mason wouldn't want you to think he was advising you as an attorney while he has conflicting interests because he'd be guilty of unprofessional conduct.

"And now, good night, Mr. Mason, and I hope you enjoy the floor show."

"Thank you," Mason said. "I'm quite certain that I will, Lieutenant, and I hope *you* enjoy *your* visit here."

Chapter Eleven

THE PHONE was ringing as Mason opened the door of his bungalow.

The lawyer kicked the door shut, hurried across to the telephone and picked it up at the end of the third ring.

"Hello," he said.

"There's a long-distance call for Mr. Perry Mason from Los Angeles," the operator said.

"This is Mr. Mason talking."

"Just a moment."

Almost at once Mason heard Paul Drake's voice on the line. "Hi, Perry."

"Hello, Paul. How did you locate me?"

"Detective work and deduction," Drake said. "I knew you were headed for Las Vegas, that Genevieve Hyde worked in the place where you're staying, and felt sure you'd register there."

"I'm here," Mason said. "Also, Lieutenant Tragg is here."

"How did he get there?"

"Apparently followed me. After I took off for Las Vegas, Tragg telephoned the local police to pick up my trail as soon as I arrived. Then he grabbed a plane, came over here and joined them."

"They got anything?"' Drake asked.

"That's quite a question," Mason said. "Nadine Palmer was hitting the tables pretty heavy and doing a good job of it. They came down on her with a search warrant and recovered a bunch of money."

"Well, they've uncovered lots here," Drake said. "I think your clients are in a mess, Perry."

"My clients?" Mason asked.

"That's right."

"It sounded as though you had an 's' on the end of that," Mason said. "And Lieutenant Tragg keeps referring to my clients in the plural. As far as I'm concerned I only have one client in this case, and that's Morley Eden."

"I think you've got two," Drake said. "I think they're together."

"Who's together?"

"Morley Eden and Vivian Carson."

"But that's absurd," Mason said. "Good heavens, Paul, they wouldn't . . ."

The lawyer's voice trailed away as the idea germinated in his mind even while he was formulating the words pointing out its absurdity.

"Exactly," Drake said, as Mason remained silent.

"Go ahead, Paul," Mason said, "give me the facts. What have they uncovered?"

"They've found Loring Carson's automobile."

"Where?"

"In Vivian Carson's garage."

"You mean out at Morley Eden's house? Or . . ."

"No, in the garage at *her* apartment."

"Go on," Mason said. "Give me the facts, Paul."

"Well, all I know is that after Carson and his wife separated she went to an apartment house where each apartment has a private garage space—an underneath, two-car garage that goes with the apartment. Now, Mrs. Carson was staying there in her apartment until Saturday when she got her surveyor and crew of construction workers and went out and ran the fence right through the middle of Eden's house. Then, of course, she moved in."

"Go on," Mason said.

"Naturally she moved in on a hurry-up basis. She took what stuff she could carry in her automobile, and of course she retained possession of her Hollywood apartment. In fact, she has it on a lease."

"And that's where they found the car?'"

"That's where they found the car."

"How did they happen to go there to look for it?"

"I don't know."

"Any chance Loring Carson left it there himself?'"

"No. That's where you come in on the deal, Perry. Both of them left it there."

"You mean Loring and Vivian?"

"No, I mean Vivian and Morley Eden."

"You're sure?"

"I'm not, but the police are. They have a witness who has made a positive identification of Morley Eden."

"Just one witness?" Mason asked.

"How many do you expect on a deal of that sort?"

"It's a mistake," Mason said. "Vivian may have been mixed up in it and may have parked the car, but Morley Eden wasn't with her. That's for sure. Eyewitnesses can be mistaken lots of times."

"I know," Drake said, "but there are certain things to keep in mind. Vivian Carson was all mixed up in this divorce case with charges of weekend trysts and all that. In the minds of the neighbors she became a scarlet woman".

"What does that have to do with it?" Mason asked.

Drake said, "You know one woman always likes to spy on an erring sister. It's an interest that's composed partially of curiosity, partially of envy, and—"

"Forget the philosophy," Mason said, "even if it *is* your nickel that's paying for the call."

"Oh, but I'm putting it on my expense account," Drake said, "and I like to philosophize."

"Well, I don't. Things are moving too fast. What happened?'"

"This neighbor heard Vivian's garage door being raised. She rushed to the window to see what Vivian was up to and whether Vivian was alone. She saw Vivian and a man she identifies as Morley Eden. Vivian parked the car. Morley Eden was running around helping her very solicitously. Then he lowered the garage door, she locked

Micronite filter.
Mild, smooth taste.
For all the right reasons.
Kent.

America's quality cigarette.
King Size or Deluxe 100's.

it, and they walked rapidly away. That car they drove into the garage was Carson's missing auto."

"That's fine," Mason said. "That gives them a good case against Eden and Vivian Carson, and now they've got a good case against Nadine Palmer. We'll see how many more murderers Lieutenant Tragg can uncover at this end."

"Be careful *you* aren't one," Drake said jokingly. "When are you coming back, Perry?"

"Sometime tomorrow morning. I'm hoping they'll turn Nadine Palmer loose after they've given her a shakedown at Headquarters."

"Now that they've found Loring's car they won't hold her," Drake said. "They'll drop her like a hot potato. They won't want the newspapers to get hold of the fact they had another suspect."

"Now that," Mason said, "is a whale of an idea. Particularly since I'm not representing Nadine Palmer in any way, I don't owe her a thing. Thanks for the suggestion."

"What suggestion?" Drake asked.

"Yours," Mason said. "Ring up the wire services. Tell them that you have a hot tip on a news story, that Las Vegas police have just picked up Nadine Palmer and that she's held for questioning in connection with the murder of Loring Carson. Tell them to check with their Las Vegas office. Don't give them your name. Tell them it's just a tip. Be sure they get Nadine Palmer's name right and then hang up.'"

"Okay," Drake said, "can do. Anything else, Perry?"

"That's enough for a while," Mason said. He put down the receiver, ran exploring fingers over the angle of his jaw, picked up the telephone, asked for the bell captain and said, "This is Perry Mason in two-o-seven. I've got to have some overnight things; an electric razor, toothbrush, hairbrush and comb, and—"

Abruptly he stopped, his eyes fixed on a dark brown briefcase at the far end of the room.

"Yes, Mr. Mason," the bell captain said, "was there something else?"

"I'll call you back in a moment," Mason said, "but start lining up those thing for me, if you will."

113

"We may not be able to get the brand of electric razor you'd like. We—"

"That's all right," Mason said. "Get whatever one is available or get a safety razor and a shaving cream dispenser. I'll call you back."

"We'll be working on it," the bell captain said.

Mason hung up, crossed to the briefcase, picked it up and looked at it.

It was a good grade of heavy leather, dark brown in color, was unlocked, and in gilt letters underneath the hasp was the printed name, "P. MASON."

Mason snapped the catch, opened the briefcase and looked inside.

The interior was well filled with an orderly array of folded documents.

Mason pulled out one of the documents. It was a bond in the sum of five thousand dollars, issued by a uitlity company and payable to A. B. L. Seymour.

The lawyer quickly riffled through the contents of the briefcase, not taking the papers out individually but making enough of a survey to realize that the briefcase was crammed with negotiable securities, all issued to A. B. L. Seymour, and apparently all of them were endorsed in blank with the signature of A. B. L. Seymour.

Mason closed the briefcase, returned to the telephone and once more called the bell captain and identified himself. "How about baggage?" he asked. "Could I get any at this time of night?"

"Oh, yes. There's a luggage shop here in the building. It stays open until quite late."

"That fine," Mason said. "I want a suitcase and a briefcase. I want each stamped with the name 'P. MASON' in gold letters.

"I want toilet articles and I'm in a terrific hurry. Will you see what you can do?"

"Right away. You want the name 'P. MASON' stamped in gold?"

"That's right."

"Would you prefer to have it 'PERRY MASON'?"

"No. I want 'P. MASON.' And spend whatever money

you need to get a rush job. I'll go to thirty dollars in tips alone.'"

"Thank you, Mr. Mason, we'll get busy."

The lawyer jiggled the phone, got the operator and placed a long-distance call to Della Street at her apartment.

"In bed, Della?" he asked when he heard her voice on the line.

"Heavens, no. I was reading. How are things coming over there?"

"Not too hot," Mason said. "I'm running into a frame-up of some sort."

"What do you mean?" she asked, her voice quick with alarm.

"I don't know," Mason told her, "but somebody is planting evidence in this case and someone has planted evidence on me."

"What sort of evidence?"

"I don't want to tell you over the phone."

"Who planted it?"'

"Probably the murderer," Mason said. "And because it couldn't have been Morley Eden or Vivian Carson, it must have been someone else.

"Now it *could* conceivably have been Nadine Palmer, in which event she's a very smart, very clever, very dangerous operator. If it wasn't she, I just don't have any idea who it could have been unless it was Genevieve Hyde, and she gives me the impression of being straightforward and frank."

"The straightforward, frank ones are the dangerous ones," Della said.

"I know it," Mason told her. "She's an actress. She makes her living by putting on a good show. She gets a man all enthused over the idea of gambling. She builds him up to a point where it's easy come, easy go, and then when things go the other way she encourages him to keep on plunging until he's had enough. By that time she manages very adroitly to withdraw herself from the picture so that there are no hard feelings."

"That," Della Street said, *"is* a job!"

"It is," Mason said, "but she has help; very expert

feminine help that is working in a combination they understand perfectly. They have all the coordinated skill of a football team making a trick play to open up the enemy's lines."

"And someone has turned that combination loose on you?"

"Someone has turned that combination loose on me," Mason said.

"I think I'd better get over there and look around," she said. "Don't you think you could use me?"

"I know I could use you," Mason told her, "but there won't be time for you to get here. If I can get rid of the hot stuff that has been dumped in my lap as a part of this frame-up I'll be on my way back to Los Angeles before you arrive. My bungalow number is two-o-seven. If you don't hear from me by morning, start checking."

"Okay," she said, "but I wish I could get there and give you some feminine support. It takes a woman to undo the machinations of another woman. A man is helpless as a fly trapped in the gossamer of a spider web."

"You sound almost poetic," Mason told her.

"I don't mean to be. I'm trying to frighten you. I could get there by midnight or soon after and——"

"The situation here will come to a head before that," Mason said. "I'll probably be on my way back by that time, unless I'm in jail."

"Take care of yourself," she pleaded.

"I'll do my best," he promised, and said good night.

The lawyer remained in his room, impatiently pacing the floor, looking at his wristwatch a dozen times every ten minutes.

At length the phone rang. Mason hurriedly picked it up.

"Hello."

"Mr. Mason?"

"Yes."

"This is the bell captain. I'll be right down with the things. We have everything."

"That's fine," Mason told him.

A few moments later the bell captain arrived with a

116

suitcase, opened it and removed a briefcase and a small nylon toilet kit.

"I just had to use my judgment, Mr. Mason," he said. "I—"

"Fine," Mason told him. "How much does it amount to?"

"We have one hundred and one dollars and thirty-five cents here. Now, if that's satisfactory . . ."

"That's quite satisfactory," Mason said, handing him a hundred-dollar bill and a fifty-dollar bill, "and I certainly appreciate all you've done."

"Thanks a lot," the bell captain said. "If that luggage isn't satisfactory . . ."

"But it is," Mason said, inspecting the luggage. "It's just what I wanted. I'm glad that you were able to get the lettering done tonight.'"

"Caught them just as they were closing up," the captain said. "They keep open at night, you know. That's when most of the curios are sold, and the luggage store is part of the curio shop. Thank you *very* much, Mr. Mason. If there's anything else we can do for you, just let us know."

"I will," Mason promised.

Mason opened the briefcase he had found in his room, transferred the negotiable securities to the new briefcase, put the empty briefcase in the new suitcase, locked the suitcase, put the key in his pocket and sauntered out to the casino, aware that the plainclothes detective was following only a few feet behind.

After a few moments at the tables the young woman who had pressed against him when she was making her bets came over toward him with eyes sparkling.

"I just wanted to say thanks."

"For what?" Mason asked.

"For luck. My, but you brought me luck! I was having hard sledding until I came over to where you were standing and . . . Well, I got off balance and . . ." She paused, smiled and said, "Then I brushed against you—against your arm . . .'"

"I remember," Mason said.

"Well, that contact certainly brought me luck," she said.

"Perhaps I could bring you some more," Mason told her.

"I've had plenty for one evening."

"How about a drink?"

"That could probably be arranged," she said archly but with invitation in her eyes.

"You come here often?" Mason asked, leading her to the bar.

"I'm here most of the time," she said. "I can't stay away from gambling. How did *you* do tonight?"

"Fairly well," Mason told her. "Nothing spectacular."

"Well, you certainly can give a person luck by induction."

"It was a pleasure to me," Mason said.

She laughed nervously. "I brushed against you rather intimately."

The waiter stood at their table.

"A Scotch and soda, Bob," she said.

"A gin and tonic for me," Mason ordered.

When the waiter had left, Mason turned to her. "My name is Mason," he said.

"How do you do, Mr. Mason? I'm Paulita Marchwell."

"You live here?" Mason asked.

"In Las Vegas."

"And the tables have a fatal fascination for you?"

"I love it here. I just love the place, the atmosphere, the people, the action—the whole thing. I guess gambling is in my blood.

"However, let's talk about you. You don't live here, do you? You have 'big businessman' stamped all over you, only you're different from most of the businessmen. There's an alert something about you . . . You're not a doctor? . . . You . . . Good Heavens! *Is* your first name *Perry?*"

Mason nodded.

"Perry Mason, the famous lawyer!" she exclaimed. "Good Lord, I should have known—there's something outstanding about you, something that creates the impression of being a tower of strength. Now that sounds very sophomoric, Mr. Mason, but . . . Well, I'm going to make a confession. I had noticed you earlier in the evening. Weren't you with some woman?"

"One of the hostesses here, I believe. A Miss Hyde."

"Oh, Genevieve," she said. "I . . ."

She paused and laughed.

"Why the light laughter?" Mason asked.

"I know her well."

"Friends?"

"Not exactly. Speaking acquaintances. And—well, I guess you *could* call it friends in a way. We . . . we get along."

The waiter brought their drinks.

"Here's to you," Mason said.

She clicked glasses with the lawyer. Her eyes, enormous under her short, gamin haircut, looked over the rim of the glass with appreciation she made no attempt to disguise.

"Have you lived here long?" Mason asked.

She said nervously, "I came here for the cure."

"The cure?" Mason asked.

"You know. The six-weeks' cure. Live here six weeks, establish a residence, get rid of your marital mistake and be on your way to commit fresh follies.

"However, in my case I liked it here so well that I just stayed on. You get to know the place and the people and—well, it's fascinating, Mr. Mason, completely, utterly fascinating."

"Then," Mason said, "you're Mrs. Marchwell, rather than—"

"Paulita, to you," she said, flashing him a sultry glance. "What are you here for, Mr. Mason? Business?"

"In a way," Mason said.

"Not business involving Genevieve, is it?"

"It's hard to say who may become involved."

"Genevieve," she said, "is *quite* a girl."

"She seems to be."

"She goes overboard every now and then."

"You mean for some man?"

She nodded.

Mason waited.

"Some big-shot contractor from Los Angeles made a

119

play for her and she was crazy about him and then he—— Well, he kept making passes at me and I think Genevieve is furious."

Mason's eyes narrowed. "The name wouldn't be Carson, would it?"

She stiffened abruptly. Her eyes changed expression. Her countenance became a poker face of immobility.

"Well?" Mason asked.

"How did *you* know?"

"My business concerns Carson, in a way."

"In what way?"

"He's dead."

"Dead!"

Mason nodded. "Murdered."

"Good heavens!" Paulita exclaimed. "You . . . When did all this happen?"

"This morning sometime, or perhaps early afternoon."

For several seconds she was silent, then she heaved a deep sigh. "Well," she said, "that's the way things go. Poor Loring. He was a good guy—once a person got to understand him."

Again she lapsed into silence.

"Does Genevieve know?" she asked at length.

Mason nodded.

She said, "Genevieve was *really* wrapped up in him. She . . . So *that's* why she came back from Los Angeles so early."

"*Back* from Los Angeles?" Mason asked, instantly attentive.

She nodded.

"You mean Genevieve was in Los Angeles today?"

"Sure. She took the plane yesterday and stayed overnight. I thought she was going to stay overnight tonight, but she was back here around four o'clock in the afternoon."

Mason's eyes narrowed.

Paulita said, "You're looking very professional, Mr. Mason. I suppose it's because she didn't tell you she'd been in Los Angeles; but I must warn you, Genevieve is one of the most secretive persons I know. When you get

120

to know her better you'll find she won't lie, but she certainly can lead you to reach false conclusions by simply keeping silent.'"

"You're sure she was in Los Angeles?" Mason asked.

"Of course I'm sure. She came back on the plane that gets in here shortly after four o'clock; four-seventeen, or four-nineteen, something like that. I saw her come in on the bus from the airport. She—"

Lieutenant Tragg's voice said, "I'm *very* sorry to interrupt, Perry, but another matter has come up. Now, you've already met Sergeant Camp. And this is Miss . . ."

Tragg turned inquiringly to the young woman.

"Marchwell," Mason said. "This is Miss Marchwell. There was something that you wanted, Lieutenant?"

"I'm sorry, I'm very sorry to bother you and it seems to me we're making confounded nuisances of ourselves, Mason, but Sergeant Camp has received an anonymous tip—one of those things that are the nightmare of all police investigators. However, this one is something that we can't ignore. It was a tip that was sent in over the telephone and it was— Well, we thought we'd better check it, that's all.

"We don't want to bother you, Mason, and I certainly hate to interrupt a tête-à-tête, but perhaps *you* could answer that question."

"What question?" Mason asked.

"We'd like to know if your clients, either Vivian Carson or Morley Eden, paid you a fee in negotiable securities—stocks, bonds or things of that sort."

"They did not."

"Let's get right down to brass tacks," Sergeant Camp said. "Did either of your clients give you some negotiable securities made in the name of Seymour?"

"No."

"Did your clients, either of them, ask you to do anything in connection with converting negotiable securities into cash?"

"No."

"Or are you keeping any securities for your clients, or either of them, or did they give you any instructions in

121

connection with any securities which they turned over to you either directly or indirectly?"

"No."

Tragg looked at Camp. "Mason won't lie."

"I still say we've got to investigate his room," Sergeant Camp said.

Lieutenant Tragg's eyes narrowed. "Perry Mason is truthful. He'll either run you around in circles or he'll drag a red herring across the trail, or he'll squeeze out of things some way, but if he tells you something definitely and straight from the shoulder, it's true."

"I have to investigate this tip," Sergeant Camp said doggedly.

"How do you propose to investigate it?" Mason asked.

"Would you mind stepping down to your room for a moment?"

"I'm busy at the moment."

"That's quite all right," Tragg said. "We'll sit down over here at a table and when you're finished we'll go on down to your room. Or perhaps you'd like to let us have your key and—"

"You got a warrant?" Mason asked.

"We don't really need a warrant," Camp said, "but we can get one. This is a public hotel and the management is always willing to cooperate."

"My baggage isn't public," Mason said, "but I'm willing to cooperate. However, I don't want to leave . . ."

Paulita Marchwell said hurriedly, "No, no. You go with the gentlemen, Mr. Mason. I certainly don't want to interfere in anything of *this* sort."

She smiled at Sergeant Camp. "I know the Las Vegas police would want to cooperate with me in every way, and I want to cooperate with them."

She got to her feet, gave Mason her hand. "Nice to have met you, Mr. Mason. Perhaps I can see you again under other circumstances when you can—have more time."

She gave him a significant look, turned and floated away.

Mason pushed back his unfinished drink and said,

"Well, you fellows certainly seem to have spoiled things for me there."

"You can always begin again where you left off," Sergeant Camp told him. "Let's go."

Mason said, "All my baggage is here in my room."

"You came over here in a hurry, didn't you, Mason?" Tragg asked.

"I do many things in a hurry."

"You bring any baggage?"

Mason said, "All my baggage is here in my room."

Tragg said, "Well, we'll only detain you a moment, Mason. We have an anonymous tip that you have a briefcase full of securities that were the property of Loring Carson, a briefcase with the words 'P. MASON' stamped on it. You carried it here from Los Angeles."

Mason said nothing.

Sergeant Camp saw and pounced on the briefcase.

"Here it is," he said to Lieutenant Tragg.

Tragg's eyes narrowed. Then he looked at Mason, then back to Camp.

"Open it," he said.

Sergeant Camp opened it.

"So you say he's truthful!" he exclaimed.

"Well, I'll be damned," Tragg said. "This is the first time I've ever known him to tell a lie."

"What do you mean a lie?" Mason asked. "You didn't ask me if I had a briefcase filled with securities. You asked me if I had securities given me by either Vivian Carson or Morley Eden. Every one of your questions related to securities I had received from them."

"Okay, okay," Tragg said. "Let's agree that my questions may have been misleading. Now where *did* you get these securities?"

"I can't tell you."

"What do you mean by that?"

"Simply that I can't tell you."

"Nuts to all that stuff," Camp said. "You can do whatever you want to, Tragg, but I wouldn't believe this guy on oath. We're taking this briefcase."

"Inventory the contents," Mason said.

123

"Nuts," Camp repeated. "We'll take the inventory at Headquarters. Come on, Tragg."

The two officers marched out of the room, taking the briefcase with them.

Mason walked over to pick up the phone. "When's the next plane to Los Angeles?" he asked.

Chapter Twelve

PERRY MASON sat with Morley Eden in the attorneys' visiting room at the jail.

"If I'm to be your attorney, Morley," he said, "you *have* to tell me what happened."

Morley Eden looked at him with anguished eyes. "I can't do it, Mason."

"Nonsense. You can always tell your attorney anything."

Eden shook his head.

"Why not?"

"It's too damned . . . In the first place, if you knew the true facts in the case you wouldn't believe them, and in the second place you wouldn't represent us."

"Did you kill him?"

"No."

"Do you know who did?"

"No."

"But you want me to represent you and Vivian Carson?"

"Yes. We're going to be indicted by the Grand Jury. We'll be jointly charged with first-degree murder, and they're going to make out one hell of a case, Mason, I'll tell you that. They're going to make out a case by circumstantial evidence that—I don't know if you *can* beat it."

Mason said, "That's all the more reason why you should tell me what actually happened. I have to know what I'm up against. The best defense to circumstantial evidence, provided, of course, that a man is innocent, is the truth."

"I tell you," Eden said, "the truth isn't going to help you. It would give you a hopeless case. As long as they're relying on circumstantial evidence you're going to have to go in there and try to beat it. I don't know how much they have. They may have a little or they may have a lot. If they have all of it we're lashed to the mast. We'll *never* get out of the mess. Your only hope, our only hope, is that they don't have all of it. We were trapped by circumstances. I can't even discuss it."

"Why do you want me to represent Vivian Carson?" Mason asked.

"Because we're going to be charged together in an indictment."

"That doesn't make any difference," Mason said. "If you didn't kill him, perhaps Vivian Carson did, and I don't want my hands tied in your defense by—"

"No, no, no, Vivian didn't kill him. I know that. I swear it."

"How do you she didn't?"

"Because she was . . . Because I *know*."

Mason regarded the man with thoughtful eyes. "Look here, Morley," he said, "is there any chance that you think you're in love with Vivian Carson?"

Morley Eden met his eyes. "I know I'm in love with her, Mason. It's something that I never thought could happen to me. It's one of the most devastating emotional storms I ever experienced. I . . . I can't begin to tell you what she means to me or how it happened. It just hit me—well, from the first minute I saw her.

"And that's one of the things that you're going to have to take into consideration. After all, she and Loring Carson were still married. There had been a divorce decree but it was only an interlocutory judgment. The interlocutory would have to run for six months before there would be a final dissolution of the marriage. The prosecution

125

will use my love for her as a motivation for the murder of her husband."

"When did all this happen?" Mason asked.

"What?"

"Your falling in love with her."

"Almost from the first time I saw her."

"That, as I remember it," Mason said, "was when she was in a very abbreviated bikini."

"All right, it was," Eden said. "And she seemed—well, there was something essentially feminine about her, a daintiness, a grace, a— She was a vision of loveliness."

"You were lonely," Mason said. "You'd been a widower, you'd been living by yourself. You came to your house, found a fence running through it. You opened the door, went into the house trying to find what in the world had happened, and there you found this woman, this vision of loveliness, as you call it. Then a little later you saw her by the pool, taking a sunbath in a bikini.

"She had quite evidently planned the whole thing: the setting, the discovery, the bikini she was wearing—probably even the lighting effect. She knew about when you were due back. She wanted you to—"

"All right, suppose she did," Eden said. "You know what she wanted at the time. She wanted me to file suit against Loring Carson. She wanted to try and discover some of the hidden assets which she was satisfied he'd been concealing in preparation for the divorce action. She has told me all about it. She intended to get me to make a pass at her and then take me before the court on contempt proceedings—in case I didn't file suit against Loring Carson."

"All right," Mason said, "go on. Tell me about the development of this emotional storm."

"The next morning she was nice to me. She handed me coffee through the fence and . . ."

"And you started to get acquainted?" Mason asked.

"Yes. It was just a start."

"Then what?"

"Then you came out and she staged that lingerie show and hang it, Mason, the thing appealed to me. The gameness of the woman; her ingenuity; the way she was fighting back with the cards stacked against her. I was there in the house and after the party was over—well, she pulled back those silly curtains and I was in the living room and I looked at her and suddenly started laughing, and then *she* began to laugh and then we sat and visited for—well, it was a long time."

"How long?"

"Until the small hours of the morning, if you want to know."

"And you knew you were in love with her?"

"Yes."

"Did you tell her so?"

"Now look, Mason, that has nothing to do with the case; but as a matter of fact, I . . ."

"Did you or didn't you?" Mason asked, as Eden hesitated.

"I didn't," Eden said, "but she could tell that I was tremendously interested in her and I realized that I was drawing out a side of her that had lain dormant for a long time. She had been the victim of a terribly unhappy marriage. She had been married to a louse, a heel, a—"

Mason held up a warning hand. "The man is dead. You're going to be accused of murdering him. Don't cultivate that type of thinking."

"I don't care," Eden said. "That's what he was. He was a louse. Here he was, married to Vivian, and he was neglecting her, running around with another woman and, in place of going to her frankly and telling her what had happened and that he wanted his freedom and trying to give *her* an opportunity to salvage something of *her* life, making a fair division of the community property and doing what should have been done under the circumstances, he started trying to cheat her out of what was rightfully hers. He hired a detective under such circumstances that—well, it may have been an innocent mistake, but I'm inclined to think he deliberately framed the whole business so he would have some excuse for blackening her name in the press, ruining her reputation. Then he started concealing assets, juggling things around so that no one could tell anything about his net worth and—"

"All right," Mason said, "all right. It's plain to be seen

127

that you're looking at the entire situation through her eyes."

"I am," Eden said, "because her eyes have the true perspective."

Mason said, "When the prosecution gets all that it will have a swell motive. Now I want to know what happened. I want to have it so you can go on the witness stand if you have to and—"

"Let me tell you this, Mason," Morley Eden said, "please believe me. I tried something and it didn't work. I thought I could outsmart the police. It was perhaps the most ghastly decision I ever made in my life. It's got us both in a situation where we'll be crucified by what we have done.

"Now then, so far it's only circumstantial evidence. I understand a good lawyer can beat a case of circumstantial evidence."

"It depends on the evidence," Mason said.

"Well, there's always a chance as long as the case is based on circumstantial evidence alone, but the minute we go on the stand and tell our story we're crucified. You'd *never* stand a chance of getting us off then. No lawyer would."

Mason said, "I'll do this much, Eden. I'll stay with the case until I find out what the evidence is against you. If at the close of the prosecution's case I decide that you're going to have to go on the stand, then you're going to have to tell me your story and then you're going to have to go on the witness stand."

"Will there be time for all that?"

"I'll be able to have a brief adjournment from the time the prosecution finishes with its case and the time we have to start putting on the defense," Mason said. "I'll take your case with the understanding that if, at that time, I think the case against you is too strong to be knocked out of court without your testimony, you'll then tell me exactly what happened."

"All right," Eden said, "it's a deal."

He reached out and gave the lawyer his hand. "The only thing is," he said, "you're to go up to that point simply looking for weak places in the prosecution's case

128

and not feeling in the back of your mind that you're going to rely on what Vivian and I can tell you."

Mason shook hands. "It's your funeral," he said. "And I mean that literally."

Chapter Thirteen

JUDGE NEDLEY C. FISK, a benevolent-appearing gentleman with a mind as sharp as a razor, glanced at Morrison Ormsby, one of the more deadly competent members of the district attorney's trial staff.

"The peremptory is with the People," Judge Fisk said.

Ormsby, intently studying a series of cabalistic notes marked opposite the names of the prospective jurors, said without looking up, "The People pass their peremptory at this time."

Judge Fisk looked at Perry Mason. "The peremptory is with the defendant."

Mason arose and said gravely, "The defendants are completely satisfied with this jury, Your Honor."

Ormsby, caught by surprise, looked up incredulously. The defense in an important murder case had not exercised a single peremptory challenge.

"Swear the jury," Judge Fisk directed the clerk.

After the jury had been sworn, Judge Fisk said, "The remaining members of the panel are excused from this courtroom.

"The persons who now compose this jury are warned that they are not to form or express any opinion in regard to the merits of this controversy until it is finally submitted to them. They are not to discuss the evidence in this case, nor are they to permit it to be discussed in their presence. Court is going to take a fifteen-minute recess before starting evidence in the case. Court will reconvene at exactly ten o'clock."

Judge Fisk left the bench.

Mason turned to where Paul Drake and Della Street were seated beside him.

"Well," he said, "this is a lawyer's nightmare. I'm going to listen to the evidence without having the faintest idea of what the prosecution is holding up its sleeve until they start throwing punches."

"You can't get a word out of the defendants?" Drake asked, looking over to where Morley Eden and Vivian Carson were seated between two officers.

"Not a word," Mason said.

"Well, the prosecution has got something all right," Drake said. "They're keeping it buttoned up, but Ormsby is as snug as a bug in a rug."

"I know," Mason said, "but he doesn't want to be *too* sure. I'm going to use every psychological trick that I can. I'm going to keep within the letter of the law but I'm going to make him prove these defendants guilty beyond all reasonable doubt.

"This is a case that is going to depend almost entirely on circumstantial evidence. It is a rule of circumstantial evidence, a rule of law in this state, that if the circumstances can be explained by any reasonable hypothesis other than that of guilt, the jurors are bound on their oaths to accept that hypothesis, and acquit the defendants.

"That is of course merely another way of stating the rule of law that a defendant can't be convicted unless the evidence proves him guilty beyond all reasonable doubt. If there is a reasonable doubt in the minds of the jurors they must resolve that doubt in favor of the defendants, and acquit.

"However, the rule has a peculiar application in regard to circumstantial evidence and I propose to rely on it."

Della Street said, "The newspaper reporter who said you were going to rely on technicalities—was that what he meant?"

"He didn't know what he meant," Mason said. "He was trying to get some copy and he was mad because I wouldn't outline to him what my defense was going to be."

"Well, that's the spirit of the law," Drake said. "A defendant doesn't have to prove himself not guilty, the prosecution has to prove him guilty beyond all reasonable doubt. A defendant can simply sit quiet and rely on his presumption of innocence to see him through."

Judge Fisk returned to the bench. The jurors took their seats. The press, having played up the house divided by barbed wire and the two defendants who had supposedly been mortal enemies but now were jointly charged with murder, had made the story one of the big crime pieces of the year.

By this time it was well known that Mason was, to use the expression, "going it blind," that his clients were not making any statements to anyone, had made none to the press and didn't intend to make any.

Some of the reporters had intimated that this was simply masterly strategy on Mason's part and that the defendants were following their attorney's instructions. Others, however, were convinced that Mason was as much in the dark about the defendants' side of the case as anyone—a situation which brought sex, mystery, drama and an unusual setting into a murder case and resulted not only in a jam-packed courtroom but in a crowded corridor where people waited, hoping that by standing in line during the morning they might have some chance of getting into the courtroom in the afternoon.

"Does the prosecution wish to make an opening statement?" Judge Fisk asked.

Ormsby nodded, arose and said, "May it please the Court, and you ladies and gentlemen of the jury, this is going to be one of the briefest opening statements I have ever made.

"The decedent, Loring Carson, and the defendant, Vivian Carson, were husband and wife. They weren't getting along, Vivian Carson sued for divorce.

"In the meantime, Morley Eden, the other defendant, hired Loring Carson to build a house for him. That house was built upon two lots which the defendant, Eden, purchased from Loring Carson.

"I won't go into all of the legal difficulties, but it turned out that of the two lots on which the house was built the decedent, Loring Carson, owned one as his separate

131

property and the defendant, Vivian Carson, owned the other as her separate property. When the title was adjudicated Vivian Carson placed a fence along her boundary, dividing the house into two parts. The defendant, Morley Eden, having a deed from Loring Carson, owned the other side of the house.

"Each defendant had a grievance against Loring Carson: Vivian Carson, because she felt her husband had been secreting money in such a manner that she couldn't get a fair accounting in the divorce action. As the evidence will show, this suspicion was justified.

"Morley Eden had purchased lots from the decedent, Loring Carson, and had paid him to build a house on those lots. He found out that Carson had lied to him as to the title and that as a result Morley Eden's house was partially built on property which did not belong to him.

"We are going to show that Loring Carson *did* have assets which he had been concealing and that he *had* arranged to conceal those assets in a place where he felt they would not be discovered—in a secret receptacle by the swimming pool of the house he was building for Morley Eden.

"By an ironic twist of fate, it turned out that of the two lots, the one awarded to the defendant, Vivian Carson, as her sole and separate property, contained the place of concealment for Loring Carson's undisclosed assets.

"Loring Carson went to the premises and opened this secret place of concealment on the fifteenth day of March of this year. He evidently intended to leave his concealed assets right where they were, feeling that no one would ever suspect that his hiding place was actually right under the very eyes of his estranged wife.

"However, he was too confident. The defendants found his hiding place, and killed Loring Carson, either in cold blood or in an altercation which followed the finding of his hiding place.

"The defendant, Vivian Carson, waited until her ex-husband had betrayed the place of concealment, then, entirely nude, she emerged from the Morley Eden side of the house, while Eden stood guard. She swam under the barbed-wire fence and withdrew an unknown amount of cash and securities valued at more than a hundred and fifty thousand dollars from this hiding place. The securities were found in the possession of Perry Mason on the day of the murder.

"Loring Carson discovered what was happening and was killed by the defendants.

"The Court will instruct you that once it has been established that a defendant, any defendant, has killed another human being, the burden of proof shifts to that defendant to prove any circumstances by way of extenuation or justification.

"It is true that we expect to establish our case in part by circumstantial evidence. Circumstantial evidence, however, is good evidence. We will show you beyond any question of doubt, by circumstantial evidence alone, that the defendants, acting together, killed Loring Carson and then attempted to conceal the evidence of their crime.

"The People of this State ask only justice at your hands.

"Thank you."

Ormsby walked back to his chair and sat down with the air of a man who is doing a disagreeable duty but intends to do it most competently.

Mason waived any opening argument at that time.

Then Ormsby, working with calm, dispassionate efficiency, his manner as thoroughly professional as that of a surgeon performing a difficult operation, started a procession of witnesses to the stand.

First he called an autopsy surgeon who testified that in his opinion Loring Carson had been dead anywhere from three to five hours when he made his examination. He placed the time of death as being between 10:30 A.M. and 12:30 P.M. on the fifteenth day of March.

Death, in the opinion of the autopsy surgeon, had been almost instantaneous, produced by a stabbing wound from a knife with an eight-inch blade. The wound had penetrated the heart muscle, but there had been a relatively small external hemorrhage, most of the bleeding being internal.

In the opinion of the autopsy surgeon the decedent had

133

not moved from the time he was stabbed until death resulted, other than to collapse in his tracks and sprawl out on the floor.

Ormsby next introduced certified copies of the interlocutory judgment disposing of the property and awarding one of the lots on which the house had been built to Vivian Carson, the other lot to Loring Carson. He introduced a certified copy of the restraining order, restraining Loring Carson, his representatives, agents or assigns, from trespassing in any way on the property set aside to Vivian Carson.

Ormsby next called the surveyor, who testified briefly that he had been called by Vivian Carson; that he had been asked to have everything in readiness so that he could leave at a moment's notice on a Saturday morning; that Vivian had called him, had had a locksmith who had opened the doors and made keys for the locks on her side of the house; that she had then instructed him to survey a line which was two inches inside her property line; that a construction crew had been waiting and that as soon as he had run a line through the house which was two inches inside of the line of property awarded to Vivian Carson, she had instructed the contractors to start stringing the fence.

The witness stated that he had remained on the job until the fence was completed, checking it with his transit; that he had gone to the opposite side of the house and had surveyed a line just two inches inside of the property line and had seen that when the fence was carried through the house the wire remained a uniform distance of two inches inside the property line.

"Did this defendant, Vivian Carson," Ormsby asked the witness, "make any statement to you at that time as to why she desired the fence line to be kept two inches inside of her property line?"

"She did."

"What did she say?"

"She said that if Morley Eden so much as put a finger on that fence it would constitute a trespass and a violation of the restraining order and she intended to have him cited for contempt."

134

"Did she make any statement indicating how she felt toward the decedent, her former husband?"

"She said she hated the ground he walked on."

"Did she make any other statement?"

"She said that he was a heel and a louse and nothing would give her greater satisfaction than to stick a knife in his ribs."

Ormsby glanced significantly at the jury. "Would the witness mind repeating that last statement?" he asked. "What was it she said?"

"That nothing would give her greater satisfaction than to stick a knife in his ribs."

"You may cross-examine," Ormsby said.

Mason smiled at the witness. "Have you had any experience with divorce?" he asked.

"Not personally."

"Among your friends?"

"Yes."

"You've known other women who have obtained divorces from their husbands?"

"Yes."

"And talked with some of them shortly after the divorce was granted, and while they were still in a bitter frame of mind?"

"Yes, sir."

"Offhand," Mason said, smiling affably, "about how many of these people have made statements to the effect that they'd like to stick a knife in their ex-husband or that he was a heel and a louse, or that they'd like to scratch his eyes out, or words to that effect?"

"Just a moment, just a moment," Ormsby said, "that's objected to as incompetent, irrelevant and immaterial and not proper cross-examination. This witness isn't an expert on divorce actions and I didn't try to qualify him as such."

Mason said, "I think if the Court please, it's proper cross-examination. Of course if the prosecutor is afraid to have him answer the question I'll withdraw it."

Judge Fisk said, "That last remark is uncalled for."

"I'm not afraid to have him answer the question,"

Ormsby bristled. "I'm simply trying to keep the record straight."

Judge Fisk said, "Well, I think I'll sustain the objection. I doubt if it's proper cross-examination. Are there any further questions?"

Mason, still smiling affably at the witness, said, "When the defendant, Vivian Carson, made that statement about wanting to stick a knife into her husband, did the tone of her voice differ in any way from any other similar comments you have heard from friends who had been divorced; comments such as 'I'd like to scratch his eyes out,' or, 'if he ever comes around me again I'll kill him,' or words to that effect?"

"Now just a moment," Ormsby said. "This is objected to as not proper cross-examination and on the same grounds as the other question and on the further ground that the Court has already ruled on the matter and that Counsel is guilty of misconduct and contemptuous conduct in trying to pursue this matter after the ruling."

Judge Fisk thought for a moment, then slowly shook his head. "I don't think," he said, "that it's the same question which was presented before. This question goes as to the tone of voice. I'm going to overrule the objection. The witness may answer."

The witness, grinning back at Mason, said, "It was about the same tone of voice that the others have used. I don't remember anyone stating particularly that she wanted to stick a knife in her husband, but I do remember one woman who said nothing would give her greater pleasure than to push her husband off a cliff—that is, her ex-husband."

"And this was in about the same tone?" Mason asked.

"About the same tone of voice."

"Now then," Mason said, "of all your acquaintances, how many of those women whom you have heard after a divorce action express an opinion that they'd like to push their husband off a cliff or scratch his eyes out, or words to that effect, have actually pushed their former husbands off cliffs, scratched their eyes out, or committed any act of violence as far as you know?"

136

"Objected to. Not proper cross-examination," Ormsby snapped.

"Sustained," Judge Fisk said. "I permitted inquiry about the tone of voice but I think that's as far as I'll go."

Mason turned to the jury with a smile which spoke volumes. "That's all," he said.

Some of the jurors smiled back at the lawyer.

Ormsby, enraged but coldly competent, said, "I will now call Lieutenant Tragg to the stand."

Lieutenant Tragg, an expert in presenting his story so that it impressed the jury, took the stand and testified to what he had discovered at the scene of the murder, introducing photographs of the corpse, describing the physical surroundings.

"You noticed moisture near the body?" Ormsby asked.

"Yes, sir. There were two very well-defined patches of water."

"About how big?"

"About as big as the palm of my hand."

"And what were they on?"

"They were on the waxed tile floor."

"How far from the body?"

"One of them was six and three-quarters inches from the nearest portion of the body; the other was twelve and one-half inches."

"Did you do anything about testing this moisture to see if you could determine its source?"

"I did. The moisture was carefully drawn up into pipettes and analyzed to see whether the water could have come from the swimming pool. The swimming pool had a relatively large amount of chlorination. It had been serviced early that day."

"And what did the analysis show in regard to the pools of water?"

"That they had the same content of chlorination as the water in the swimming pool."

"Have you taken photographs to show the position of the fence as it crossed the swimming pool?"

"I have."

"Will you produce those photographs, please, and also

137

all photographs which you took or which were taken under your direction showing the body, the house and the surroundings. I'd like to have the scene of the crime identified photographically so that the jurors can become oriented."

Tragg produced a folio of photographs and for the next half hour the photographs were introduced one at a time, identified by Tragg as to what was shown, position of the camera, direction in which the picture was taken, the time at which it was taken and the photograph was then introduced in evidence.

"Who was present when you were at the scene of the murder?" Ormsby asked.

"Well, Morley Eden, one of the defendants, was there, and Mr. Perry Mason, who is acting as his attorney; and later on, Vivian Carson, the other defendant appeared. There were, of course, various newspaper reporters and personnel from the police department and, later on, a deputy coroner."

"Mr. Perry Mason was there?"

"He was there."

"Did you have any conversation with him about the crime?"

"Yes."

"Did Mr. Mason make any suggestions?"

"Yes."

"What were they?"

"He suggested that I pay particular attention to the condition of the clothing of the corpse."

"What part of the clothing?"

"The sleeves of the shirt."

"What about the shirt?"

"The shirt," Lieutenant Tragg said, "was a shirt with French cuffs. The cuff links were diamond cuff links that had been covered with a black enamel so that the diamonds were concealed. A part of the enamel on the right cuff link, however, had chipped away disclosing the diamond underneath."

"Were these large or small diamonds?"

"Quite large, and quite valuable. The cuff links themselves were of platinum."

138

"And what about the shirt itself?"

"The sleeves of the shirt were wet up to the elbow."

"The corpse was wearing a coat, I believe?"

"That's right."

"And the sleeves of the coat?"

"They were not wet except on the inside where moisture from the wet shirt sleeves had soaked into the lining. However, the sleeves themselves were not wet."

"And was there any conversation with Mr. Mason concerning this?"

"There was.'"

"What did Mr. Mason say?"

"He suggested that I make an inspection of the swimming pool."

"And you did this?"

"Yes."

"And what did you find?"

"Nothing."

"Then what happened?"

"Then Mason suggested that I had not looked far enough or hard enough."

"You gathered the impression from what Mr. Mason said that in some way he was familiar with the hiding place which you subsequently discovered and wished to direct your attention to it?"

"Just a moment," Mason said. "That question is argumentative; it calls for a conclusion of the witness. It is, moreover, incompetent, irrelevant and immaterial."

"The objection is sustained," Judge Fisk said. "Surely, Mr. Prosecutor, you don't need to direct the attention of this witness as to his conclusions. Let him show what he did, what he found."

"Yes, Your Honor," Ormsby said, glancing at the jurors to make certain they had got the point.

"Let me put it this way," Ormsby went on, as though baffled by the technical barrier put up by the Court but patiently desiring to get an important matter before the jurors, "you *did* complete a survey of the swimming pool?"

"I did."

"And found nothing?"

"Nothing."

"Then you made a second search."

"Yes, sir."

"And at whose suggestion was that?"

"The suggestion of Mr. Perry Mason."

"Now, by Perry Mason, you mean the attorney who is at present representing the defendants in this action."

"Yes, sir."

"And what did Mr. Mason say—if anything?"

Ormsby got up from his chair and stood waiting for the answer, emphasizing the question by his action, and also emphasizing the answer Lieutenant Tragg was about to make.

Tragg said, "Mr. Mason suggested that I look behind the steps of the swimming pool."

"Behind the steps of the swimming pool," Ormsby repeated.

"Yes, sir."

"And you did so?"

"I did so."

"And what did you find?"

"As soon as I looked behind there, or rather, as soon as I groped behind there with my hand, I felt a small metal ring."

"And what did you do?"

"I inserted my fiinger in that ring and pulled gently."

"And what happened?"

"I could immediately feel that this ring was at one end of a flexible, metallic cable which was running over a roller."

"And what happened then?"

"I pulled the ring a matter of some two or three inches, which released a catch on the inside of a receptacle some ten feet back from the swimming pool."

"And then what happened?'"

"A spring raised up a section of tile about eighteen inches square, disclosing a cleverly concealed hiding place measuring sixteen and one-quarter inches square, and two feet, three and a half inches deep, lined with steel and containing an automatic spring catch so that when the tile was pushed down the catch would automatically lock on the tile, holding it in position."

"The tile was hinged on one end?"

"Yes, sir."

"And what, if anything, did you find in this steel-lined receptacle?"

"Nothing."

"Nothing?"

"That is right. Absolutely nothing."

"And did Mr. Mason try to register surprise when you discovered this ring in the place which he had so insistently pointed out? . . . Well, I'll withdraw that. I beg the pardon of Court and counsel. As I think it over I realize that question is improper. I just want to make sure, however, Lieutenant, that I understand your testimony correctly. You found this ring in a place that was indicated by Mr. Mason?"

"He indicated that I search there."

"And that was after you had previously explored the swimming pool and found nothing."

"Yes, sir."

Ormsby strode over to the counsel table where Mason was sitting, bent slightly forward and said, "I just want to show you, if you want to grandstand to this jury I'll meet you halfway."

"Go right ahead," Mason said in an undertone.

"Now then, this tile was pushed up by a spring?" Ormsby asked.

"It was."

"Where was that spring?"

"It was a coil spring, as we subsequently discovered, which had been inserted so that it was around the steel rod which served as an axis on which the hinge revolved. Now, that's not expressed very clearly, but the point is this tile was hinged. A half-inch steel rod ran through the hinge and furnished the pivot on which the hinge was raised. This steel spring, or coil spring, was twisted around the ends of this rod and was on a sufficient tension so that whenever the catch was released the tile raised up."

141

"This tile, I take it, was the same in appearance and dimensions as the other tiles?"

"It was identical with the other tiles, except for the fact that a hole had been drilled in the tile, a metal insert had been placed in this hole to give it reinforcement and cemented in place. Then the steel rod which acted as an axis on which the tile revolved was inserted in this piece of cemented pipe so that the whole constituted a very rugged hinge."

"And there was a spring so that the lid came up when the wire was pulled?"

"Yes, sir."

"And how could this tile, this hinged tile you have referred to, be closed?'"

"Only by physical pressure sufficient to overcome the tension of the spring.'

"Was this tile arranged so that it was virtually impossible to detect that it was different from the others?"

"It was a very cunning piece of work," Tragg said. "Even after we knew that there was a hinged tile it was possible to stand on it or walk on it and have no inkling of what lay beneath. The hinge was so carefully constructed and the spring catch was so mechanically perfect that there was absolutely no give or sway to the tile or anything to indicate that it wasn't embedded firmly in cement."

"And the receptacle was waterproof?"

"It was waterproof."

"How was this waterproofing arranged?"

"By a piece of sponge rubber covered with tape which surrounded the lower side of the lip of the hinged tile."

"So that any person pushing this hinged tile back into place would be very apt to place fingertips on this tape?"

"Yes, sir.'"

"And, once raised, the tile *had* to be pushed back into place in order to close it. Is that right?"

"Yes, sir."

"Now then, *did* you find any latent fingerprints on this tape which surrounded the lip of the tile or *did* you find any fingerprints on the interior surface of the tile—now mind you, Lieutenant, I am asking you about the interior, not the exterior—or in the interior of the steel-lined receptacle?"

"I did."

"Did you discover latent fingerprints which could be deciphered?"

"I did."

"And you developed those latent fingerprints and photographed them?"

"I did."

"You subsequently took the fingerprints of various persons whom you felt might have had access to this receptacle or to the premises on which the receptacle was located?"

"Yes, sir."

"And, by making comparison, were you able to determine who had made some of these fingerprints?"

"Yes, sir."

"Whose fingerprints were they?"

Tragg swiveled in the witness chair so that he was looking straight at the jurors. "Two of the persons who had made fingerprints on the *inside* surface of the tile and on the tape were the defendants, Vivian Carson and Morley Eden."

"You mean that you found both of their prints there?"

"I found both of their fingerprints."

"Do you have photographs of those latent prints, and photographs of the fingerprints of the defendants?'"

"I do."

"Do you have those photographs with you?"

"I have."

"Will you produce them, please?"

Tragg produced the photographs and they were introduced in evidence, a series of photographic enlargements which stood on easels while Tragg pointed out the points of similarity.

Ormsby turned from the photographs to the witness and said, "You stated that the other defendant, Vivian Carson, was present at the scene?"

"That is right. She was present at her side of the house."

"Did you go to call on her?"

"I did."

"You questioned her?"

"Yes, sir."

"And did you ask her where she had been and what she had been doing?"

"Yes, sir. She said she had been shopping and had just returned."

"Let's see if I understand the situation," Ormsby said, glancing at the jury to make sure they were following him. "The fence divided the house, running through a part of the living room and out over the swimming pool. Now, which side are the bedrooms on, the Morley Eden side or the Vivian Carson side?"

"The bedrooms are on the Eden side."

"And the kitchen?"

"That is on the Vivian Carson side."

"And as I understand it from your testimony, you went over to question Mrs. Carson, one of the defendants here?"

"That's right."

"Where did you question her?"

"In the kitchen, and later on the patio."

"And while you were in the kitchen did you have occasion to notice a magnetic bar on which knives were attached?"

"I did."

"Do you have the murder weapon in your possession?"

"I do."

"Will you produce it, please?"

Tragg produced the wooden-handled knife, and Ormsby asked that it be introduced in evidence.

"No objection," Mason said.

"Directing your attention to the time when you were in the kitchen, did you discuss the murder weapon with Mrs. Carson?"

"I did. I asked her if any knife was missing from the bar where the knives were kept, the magnetic bar just to the right of the electric range."

"And her answer to that question?"

"That there was nothing missing."

"Then what?"

144

"I directed her attention to a wooden-handled knife and asked her if that had been there all the time and she said it had. I then got the knife and found that it had never been used; that is, that it still had a crayon price mark on the blade."

"Did you direct her attention to that?"

"I did, yes, sir."

"And what was her answer?"

'She said that it had never been used to her knowledge; that she had only been in the house a short time."

"Do you have that knife with you, that second knife?"

"I do."

"Will you produce it, please?"

Tragg produced the second knife and it, too, was introduced in evidence.

"I call your attention to these black crayon marks on the blade of this knife, Lieutenant. Were those same marks on the blade of that knife when you took possession of it?"

"They were."

"Did you make an attempt to locate the car Loring Carson owned at the time of his death?"

"We did. We secured information from the motor vehicle department, and after we had a description we put out an all-points bulletin to pick up the car."

"Did you ever find it?"

"Yes. Some hours after the discovery of the body."

"*Where* did you find it, Lieutenant?"

"In a locked garage rented by the defendant, Vivian Carson, at the Larchmore Apartments in this city."

"Did the defendants, or either of them, make any explanation as to how this car happened to be in that garage?"

"No explanation. They refused to discuss it."

"I ask that that last remark of the witness be stricken from the record," Mason said. "The defendants are not required by law to make any explanation."

"Motion denied," Judge Fisk said. "The witness has testified to a refusal which is the equivalent of testifying to a statement made by defendants."

"Was there some conversation between you and Vivian

145

Carson about Loring Carson's concealing assets in the divorce action?" Ormsby asked the witness.

"Yes. She stated several times that her ex-husband had secreted assets and had large sums of cash and securities which she had been unable to locate, and that Judge Goodwin, who had tried the divorce case, had been unable to locate. She said that Judge Goodwin had specifically stated that he was convinced that such assets existed."

"What time did this conversation take place, Lieutenant?"

"It started at about—oh, perhaps two o'clock and continued at intervals until around quarter to three o'clock."

"Did you find any assets on the body of Loring Carson?"

"We did. We found large sums of cash and—that is, they would be large in the eyes of a police officer—and we found traveler's checks in a large amount made to A. B. L. Seymour."

"Do you have those traveler's checks with you?"

"I do."

"Will you produce them, please?"

The book of checks was produced and marked in evidence and also the cash that had been found on the body.

"Now, using this name of A. B. L. Seymour on the traveler's checks as a clue, or I may say as a starting point, did you run down this A. B. L. Seymour?"

"Yes, sir."

"What did you find?"

"I found there was no such actual person as A. B. L. Seymour, that it was an alias that had been taken by Loring Carson for the purpose of concealing assets; that he had purchased large sums of traveler's checks; that he had purchased negotiable securities in the name of A. B. L. Seymour; and that he had an account in a Las Vegas bank in the name of A. B. L. Seymour; that the balance in the bank was something over a hundred thousand dollars."

"And did you check the signature of A. B. L. Seymour to make sure that it was in the handwriting of the decedent?"

"I did."

"Did you ever locate any securities in the name of A. B. L. Seymour?"

"I did."

"Where?"

"In Las Vegas."

"Where in Las Vegas?"

"In the room of a hotel bungalow which had been rented by Mr. Perry Mason."

"Indeed!" Ormsby said, pausing dramatically. "Mr. Perry Mason, eh?"

"Yes, sir."

"Were these securities in his possession?"

"Yes, sir. In a briefcase."

"A briefcase which he had been carrying with him from Los Angeles?"

"It was a briefcase which belonged to him. It was in his room in Las Vegas. I assumed he had brought it with him."

"Don't make any assumptions," Judge Fisk said. "Simply state the facts."

"I make no move to strike," Mason said. "Having made the statement as to his assumption in response to a leading question, I would like to have the entire answer remain in the record."

Judge Fisk looked searchingly at Perry Mason, then smiled. "Very well," he said, "there being no motion to strike, the answer will stand."

"And did Mr. Mason make any statement as to how he had come into possession of these securities?" Ormsby asked the witness.

"He did not."

"You took the briefcase with the securities?"

"We did."

"Was there any identifying mark on that briefcase?"

"Yes. The name of Perry Mason was stamped on it in gilt letters—that is, the name so stamped was 'P period Mason.' "

"You have that briefcase and the securities?"

"I have surrendered it to you. I believe you have it in

147

your possession, but they have my identifying marks on them."

Ormsby produced a briefcase and the stock certificates and had them identified one at a time and introduced in evidence.

"I think," he said, "this concludes my direct examination of this witness, at least for the time being; but inasmuch as it is necessary to develop this case in episodes, so to speak, I may wish to recall the witness later."

"No objection," Mason said.

"Do you wish to reserve your cross-examination until the conclusion of the testimony?" Judge Fisk asked Mason.

"I would like to ask a few questions now and then I might ask other questions later on," Mason said.

"Very well, go ahead."

"You have intimated," Mason said, "that these securities and the briefcase which you found in my possession were taken by me from my clients here in Los Angeles and taken to Las Vegas, Nevada."

"I didn't know I had intimated it," Tragg said, smiling affably. "It's what I thought—of course."

Tragg's slight hesitation before adding the words *of course,* and his smile, gave force to his point.

"Did you have any evidence that I had received those securities in Los Angeles and had taken them to Las Vegas?"

"I did not uncover any *direct* evidence," Tragg said. And then added gratuitously, "Those things are seldom done in the presence of the police, you know, Mr. Mason."

There was a ripple of laughter from the crowded courtroom.

"I think," Judge Fisk said, "that I will ask the witness to refrain from these voluntary statements and simply answer the questions. After all, Lieutenant, you're a police officer, you have been on the witness stand many times, you are familiar with courtroom procedure and you know only too well the effect of what you're doing. I feel that the hearing will be more orderly if you abide by the rules."

148

"I'm sorry, Your Honor," Tragg said.

"Proceed," Judge Fisk announced.

"Now then," Mason said, "when you started groping around the edges of the swimming pool looking for something that would be a key to the wet shirt sleeves of the decedent, did *you* get *your* shirt sleeves wet?"

"No, sir," Tragg said, "probably because I wasn't in any great hurry."

'What did that have to do with it?"

"I rolled up my sleeves."

"Both of them?"

"Yes . . . No, I'm mistaken on that, Mr. Mason. I'm sorry. I rolled up my right shirt sleeve up above the elbow."

"You didn't roll up the left sleeve."

"No."

"And didn't get it wet?"

"No. I used my right arm entirely in my explorations."

"Thank you," Mason said. "I think that's all at the moment."

"Call Oliver Ivan to the stand," Ormsby announced.

Ivan was a middle-aged individual, rather heavyset, stolid, unemotional and quietly positive.

"What is your occupation?" Ormsby asked.

"I run a hardware store."

"Were you operating a hardware store on the fifteenth of March of this year?"

"I was."

"Where?"

"Next to the Village Motion Picture Theater on Dupont Street."

"Have you ever seen the defendants before?"

"I have."

"When did you first see them?"

"The first time I can remember seeing them was on the fifteenth of March."

"At what time?"

"Sometime between twelve and twelve-thirty."

"Did you have any conversation with them?"

"Yes."

149

"Did you conclude any business transaction with them?"

"Yes."

"What was the business transaction?"

"They wanted to buy a knife."

"They were together?"

"Yes."

"Did you sell them a knife?"

"I did."

"Would you recognize that knife if you saw it?"

"I would."

"I show you People's Exhibit G and ask if that is a knife you have seen before?"

"That is the identical knife that I sold them. It has my price mark on the blade. It has both the selling price mark and my private cost mark on the blade. The letters 'EAK' represent the cost to me and the selling price of the knife is penciled on the blade."

"Was there any conversation which you overheard between the defendants as to the type of knife they wanted?"

"Yes. They conversed in low tones, but I was able to hear them perfectly. They wanted what they referred to as 'an identical knife.' "

"Did they say what it was to be identical to?"

"No. Just that they wanted a knife that was identical."

"Did you notice any peculiarity about their mannerisms?"

"The woman, Mrs. Carson, was trembling so she could hardly hold the knife. The man seemed to be rather excited, but he was trying to calm her."

"Did you notice any evidences of affection or any indication as to how they felt toward each other?"

"The man had his arm around her quite a bit of the time, patting her on the shoulder and telling her to take it easy."

"Now you say 'the man.' To whom do you refer?"

"Whenever I have said the words 'the man,' I referred to the other defendant, Morley Eden."

"You have no doubt that this is the knife that you sold them?"

"No doubt at all."

"You may cross-examine," Ormsby said.

Mason's manner was urbane, almost casual. "You ha[ve] a good-sized hardware store?" he asked.

"We carry a pretty good stock."

"This particular knife. Do you remember where y[ou] purchased it?"

"I purchased a gross of these knives on the fourth d[ay] of February from the Quality Cutlery Company. That [is] a cutlery jobber."

"Purchased a gross?" Mason asked in some surprise.

"Yes."

"And only marked the cost and selling price on t[he] blade of *one* knife?"

"I didn't say that," Ivan said sharply. "I simply sa[id] I had marked the cost and selling price on this one knife[.]"

"Did you mark it on any of the others?"

"I marked it on all of the others."

"A gross?"

"A gross."

"And put those on sale?"

"Yes."

"Then," Mason said, "as far as you know, this part[ic]ular knife could have been purchased at any time fr[om] the fourth day of February and up to the fifteenth [of] March."

"I remember selling them the knife."

"You remember selling *a* knife," Mason said. "B[ut] as far as you know *this particular knife,* with this co[st] mark and selling price on the blade, *could* have been so[ld] at any time after the fourth day of February and prior [to] the sixteenth day of March; that is, including the morni[ng] of the fifteenth of March."

"Yes, I guess so."

"It could have been bought by any person."

"That is true."

"Then as far as you can tell while you are under oa[th] Loring Carson, the decedent, could have purchased th[e] knife from you and placed it in the kitchen of the ho[me] he was equipping for Morley Eden?"

The witness shifted his position uncomfortably.

remember the conversation. I remember the transaction with these defendants.'

"You remember selling them *a* knife," Mason said affably. "You identify this knife as being one of a gross shipment you received. You can't truthfully and conscientiously go any further than that, can you?"

"No, I guess not."

"You remember selling them *a* knife," Mason went on. "I am now asking you if you can testify under oath that *this particular knife* now in evidence was not sold to Loring Carson prior to the fifteenth day of March of this year and after the fourth day of February when your shipment of one gross was received."

"No, I guess I can't," the witness said.

"That's all," Mason said cordially, "and thank you for your very commendable frankness. I have no further questions."

"I have a question on redirect," Ormsby said. "You *did* sell *these* defendants a knife on the fifteenth day of March of this year which is absolutely identical in every way with this knife which I show you and which had the same figures on the blade. Is that right or not?"

"Objected to," Mason said, "on the ground that Counsel is trying to cross-examine his own witness; on the ground that the question is leading and suggestive."

"It is leading," Judge Fisk said.

"I was simply trying to summarize his testimony," Ormsby said.

"I suggest that if Counsel is going to summarize the testimony of this witness he wait until he argues the case to the jury," Mason said.

Judge Fisk smiled. "I think that is right. Please reframe your question, Counselor."

"Oh, I have no further questions of this witness," Ormsby said irritably. "That's all."

"That's all. You may leave the stand," Judge Fisk said.

Ormsby said, "I want to call Lorraine Henley."

The woman who marched forward to the stand was in her early forties; a pinched-faced, rather slender woman with lips that were a thin line of determination.

When she had been sworn Ormsby asked, "Where do you live?"

"At the Larchmore Apartments."

"How long have you lived there?"

"Something over a year."

"Are you acquainted with the defendant Vivian Carson?"

"I am."

"Did she live near you?"

"She lived in the Larchmore Apartments, Apartment 4B. That is directly across the car area from where I live."

"Can you explain what you mean when you refer to the car area?"

"Yes. The apartments are arranged in the form of a big L on slightly sloping ground. The apartments have a street entrance fronting on two streets. There is an alley on each side of the apartment houses, and this cement car area is accessible from either of the alleys. It is a lower area than the streets on which the apartments face.

"Now, I have to explain that. The corner where the streets intersect is the highest part of the ground. The main street keeps a rather uniform level, but the side street falls off rather abruptly. However, the apartments all have garages underneath them, with the exception of the four apartments on the corner. They have separate garages."

"Was there a garage under the apartment rented by the defendant Vivian Carson?"

"There was, a double garage."

"On the fifteenth day of March did you notice the defendant Vivian Carson?"

"I did indeed."

"At what hour of the day?"

"About eleven-fifteen or eleven-thirty in the morning."

"What was she doing?"

"She was opening the door of her garage—that is, one of her garages."

"And then what happened?"

"I saw a man drive a car into the garage."

"Did you observe the man?"

153

"Very carefully.'"

"Did you ever see him again?"

"I did."

"Do you see him now?"

"I do. He is Morley Eden, one of the defendants in this case. The man sitting at that table right there."

"The one who is seated beside Vivian Carson?"

"Yes."

"And what did you observe with reference to the car?"

"Well, the man drove the car into the garage after Mrs. Carson opened the door. Then the man came out, she closed and locked the door and then the two of them walked rapidly away together."

"They didn't go into Mrs. Carson's apartment?"

"No, that is I didn't *see* them go in. There is a back entrance to the apartment house, but they walked down the car parking area to the alley and then turned out of sight."

"You may inquire," Ormsby said.

Mason's voice was almost gentle in its quiet courtesy. "What were *you* doing when the defendants were parking this car?"

"Watching them," she snapped.

There was a slight titter in the courtroom.

"And what had you been doing just before that?"

"Sitting by the window."

"Keeping an eye on the apartment rented by Vivian Carson?"

"Well, I saw it."

"Were you sitting there watching it?"

"I was sitting there at the time, yes."

"And how long had you been sitting there?"

"For some time. I don't know how long."

"All the morning?"

"A good part of the morning."

"And had you been watching the apartment the night before?"

"Well, I'd kept an eye on things."

"Why?" Mason asked.

"Because I just wondered what was going on. I guess a body is entitled to a little human curiosity. Vivian Car-

154

son had left her apartment a few days before, carrying
some suitcases, and she hadn't been back. I just won
dered where she had gone and what she had been doing.

"So you kept an eye on her apartment so you coul
find out."

"Yes."

"Now," Mason said, "you can't tell the make of th
car that these people parked in the garage, can you? Tha
is, the make and model."

"No, I can't. It was a green car. That's all I know."

"You don't know very much about the different make
of cars?"

"No, I don't."

"Do you drive a car?"

"No."

"You don't own a car?"

"No."

"Have you ever owned a car?"

"I haven't owned a car for some time. I go on the bu
to do my shopping."

"And you didn't by any chance jot down the licens
number of this car?"

"No."

"Did you notice whether it was an out-of-state license?

"I wasn't looking at the car, I was looking at th
woman and the man."

"You had taken it on yourself to become a self-ap
pointed censor of Vivian Carson's comings and goings?

"Well, I'm a decent woman. That's a decent neighbor
hood and I want to keep it that way. I'd certainly rea
enough about her in the papers to want to keep m
eyes open and see what was happening."

"Did you know whether what you had read in the pa
pers was true or false?"

"I didn't say whether it was true or false. I'd rea
about her in the papers. You wanted to know why I wa
keeping an eye on her and I've told you."

"Thank you," Mason said. "I think that covers th
situation very nicely, Mrs. Henley—or is it Miss Henley?"

"It's *Miss* Henley!" she snapped. "I said '*Miss*' whe
I gave my name to the court officer."

Mason smiled courteously but significantly and glanced at the jurors.

"Thank you very much, *Miss* Henley," he said. "I have no further questions."

"That's all," Judge Fisk said. "Call your next witness, Mr. Prosecutor."

With the manner of a man announcing a dramatic surprise which is destined to have far-reaching repercussions, Ormsby said, "At this time, Your Honor, I wish to call Nadine Palmer to the stand."

Nadine Palmer came forward and was sworn. She was wearing a teak-brown suit, a modish hat, and carried a brown leather purse. Her long legs, beautifully tan under gossamer nylons, were accented by highly polished brown shoes.

Her alert eyes were watchful as she settled herself in the witness box and looked quickly from Ormsby to Mason and back to Ormsby, then over at the jury, then once more back to the prosecutor.

"Your name is Nadine Palmer, you reside at 1721 Crockley Avenue?"

"That is right."

"Are you acquainted with either of the defendants?"

"I am not personally acquainted with either of them, no."

"Did you know Loring Carson in his lifetime?"

"I had seen him. I don't remember having talked with him, and when I say I am not personally acquainted with Mrs. Carson I do not mean to imply that I do not know her by sight. I have attended several meetings where she has been present and I know her when I see her."

"Directing your attention to the fifteenth of March of this year, I will ask you where you were on the morning of that day."

"I drove to a place known as Vista Point."

"Now, can you tell us where Vista Point is in relation to the house built by Loring Carson and sold to Morley Eden?"

"It's about a quarter of a mile—well, perhaps not that far—from the house. The site is so situated that you can look down on the back of the house—the patio, the

156

swimming pool and the property below the swimming pool."

"Is it considerably higher than the house in question?"

"Yes. I don't know just how many feet, but you can look down on the house. You can see the roof."

"Can you see the road leading up to the house?"

"No, you can't see that. You can only see the patio, the swimming pool and the rooms on that side of the house. The house itself obscures the view of the driveway on the other side and it's impossible to see the road leading to the house because that comes up a slight grade and the house shuts off the view."

"I see," Ormsby said. "Now, I have here a map showing Vista Point, and I will ask you if you will first orient yourself with this map and then point out to the jury just where you were on the fifteenth of March of this year."

After a moment the witness placed a finger on the map. "I was here," she said.

"What time was it?"

"It was about—well, I guess I got there about ten-fifteen or a little after."

"And did you wait there?"

"I waited."

"Did you have any visual aid with you?"

"I had a pair of binoculars."

"And what were you doing with those binoculars?"

"I was watching the rear of the Carson house."

"By the Carson house you mean the house that was built by Loring Carson and sold to Morley Eden?"

"Yes."

"May I ask what was your reason for being there?"

"It was a personal reason. I . . . I understood that a gentleman who resented some of the things that Loring Carson had done to my reputation was going to insist upon Carson making some sort of a retraction and if Carson was recalcitrant he intended to—well, I believe he said he intended to teach him a lesson."

"While you were there what did you see—did you see any signs of activity?"

"Yes."

"Will you describe them to the jury, please?"

157

"Well, when I first started watching there seemed to be no one home . . . and . . ."

"That can be stricken out as a conclusion of the witness," Ormsby said. "Just state what you saw. Don't give your conclusions, Mrs. Palmer—just what you saw."

"Well, I parked my car, got out and looked through the binoculars from time to time. I would look away to rest my eyes and then look back, and if I saw something I thought would interest me I raised the binoculars."

"And what was the first thing that you saw, the first motion?"

"I saw Loring Carson."

"Now, where did you see him?"

"He was on the kitchen side of the house."

"Let's get this straight as far as the record is concerned," Ormsby said. "The house was divided by a barbed-wire fence. You saw that?"

"Oh, of course."

"On one side of the barbed-wire fence was the portion of the house which contained the kitchen. On the other side of the fence was the part which contained a portion of the living room and the bedrooms."

"That is, generally speaking, correct."

"Let's refer, then, to the kitchen side of the house and the bedroom side of the house, just to keep the record straight at this point," Ormsby said. "Now, where was Mr. Loring Carson when you first saw him?"

"On the kitchen side of the house."

"You're positive?"

"I'm positive."

"What did you do, with reference to watching him?"

"I focused the binoculars on him."

"Do you know the magnification of those binoculars?"

"Eight-power."

"Could you see him clearly?"

"Quite clearly."

"You recognized him?"

"Oh, yes."

"Could you see what he was doing?"

"He bent down over the swimming pool by the steps.

158

I couldn't see what he was doing. I kept trying to focus the glasses so as to get the best adjustment possible."

"All right, what happened?"

"Mr. Carson got down on his knees by the portion of the swimming pool that was near the cement steps."

"Was he carrying anything?"

"He was carrying a leather briefcase."

"What did you see him do?"

"He got down on his knees and put his right forearm in the water of the swimming pool. I could see that he was pulling at something and then suddenly I saw a section of what apparently was solid tile open up, disclosing a receptacle underneath."

"And what did Mr. Carson do?"

"Carson took some papers from his briefcase, put them in this receptacle and closed the tile."

"Go on. What else did you see, if anything?"

She said, "Loring Carson went inside of the house and almost immediately, from the other side of the house—"

"Now, just a minute," Ormsby interrupted. "Let's keep this straight. What side of the house did Loring Carson go in, the kitchen side or the bedroom side?"

"The kitchen side."

"All right, now when you say the other side of the house, what do you mean?"

"The bedroom side of the house."

"And what happened on the bedroom side of the house?"

"A nude woman came running out of the house and went into the pool like a flash."

"You were looking through your binoculars?"

"Yes."

"Could you recognize this woman?"

"I am not able to say positively and beyond all question as to who it was, but I think—"

"Now, just a moment," Mason interrupted. "If the Court please, the witness has answered the question. She said that she couldn't identify the person. It makes no difference as to who she *thinks* the person might be if she can't swear who that person was."

"I submit that she was simply using a colloquialism,"

Ormsby said. "She means that she can identify the person to a reasonable certainty but she is trying to be fair and recognizes that there is room for the possibility of an error."

"I don't think it needs the prosecutor to interpret what the witness has stated," Mason said. "She is testifying in the English language and I think I understand the English language as well as the prosecutor."

Judge Fisk frowned thoughtfully, then said, "Let me question the witness. I would like to have Counsel refrain from interrupting me. Mrs. Palmer, you saw a person in the nude?"

"A woman. She was in the nude."

"She wasn't wearing a bathing suit?"

The witness shook her head vigorously. "She was in the nude."

"And what did she do?"

"She came streaking out of the bedroom side of the house and cut into that water so fast that it almost took my breath just watching her."

"She was running?"

"She was running and then she jumped into the water so clean she hardly made a splash and swam like a seal."

"You had the binoculars?"

"I had the binoculars but I couldn't keep her in the field of the binoculars. She was moving too fast—that is, she was within the field of the binoculars but not within the field of the center of my eyes, if you know what I mean. She was just moving—just as fast as she could go."

"Did you get a good look at this woman?"

"Only in a general way, just a blurred sort of a look."

"Could you swear absolutely as to the identity of that woman?"

"Not absolutely. I have a general fleeting impression but that's all."

"I think, under the circumstances," Judge Fink ruled, "we'll consider the statement of the witness that she *thinks* she can tell who the person was as being a common colloquialism; that we will let her testify and the question of lack of positive identification will go to the

160

weight, rather than the sufficiency of the evidence. You may continue to lay your foundation, Mr. Prosecutor."

"I'll go on a little further," Ormsby said. "This woman jumped into the pool and swam across it?"

"Like a seal. She cut through the water so fast it was incredible."

"And then what did she do?"

"She jumped up the steps at the shallow end of the pool, pulled something and the same tile flew open. She bent over the tile. She had some kind of a white plastic bag with her. She started pulling out papers and stuffing them in the bag."

"And did you get a good look at her at that time?"

"She had her back turned at that time."

"You were watching through binoculars?"

"Yes."

"Then what did you do?"

"Then," the witness said, "I realized what was happening and—"

"Never mind what you realized," Ormsby interrupted. "Please pay careful attention to the question, Mrs. Palmer. What did you *do?*"

"I tossed my binoculars onto the seat of the car and started running."

"Running where?"

"Running down a trail that came to the ground below the swimming pool of the house."

"You knew that trail was there?"

"I knew the trail was there."

"How long did it take you to run down that trail?"

"Not very long. It's—oh, I don't know, about two hundred yards, I guess, down the hill by trail and then you come to an open place and start uphill again toward the swimming pool."

"Could you see the swimimng pool or the house while you were running down the trail?"

"No. The hill is covered with brush, a chaparral I guess it is—and I believe there's some greasewood in it. I don't know just what the nature of the brush is, but it's the kind of brush that you see all over the Southern California foothills."

"And when you emerged from the brush, where were you? Can you show us on the map?"

"At about this point," the witness said, indicating a place on the map.

"I'll just mark this with a circle," Ormsby said. "Now from this point on you could see the house clearly?"

"Oh, yes."

"And what did you do?"

"I moved toward the house, moving very **rapidly**. I was somewhat out of breath but I hurried."

"And what did you see?"

"Nothing."

"What about the swimming pool?"

"It was vacant."

"What about the tile where the place of concealment had been built?"

"The tile was open; that is, the tile was standing up on its hinge."

"And what did you do?"

"I headed for the patio, but then I heard low voices coming from the house."

"You were on the bedroom side?"

"Yes."

"So what did you do?"

"I walked close to the wall of the bedroom side of the building."

"And then what?"

"Then I could distinguish what was being said."

"And what *was* being said?"

"Just a minute," Mason said, "let's first find out who is doing the talking."

"I'm coming to that," Ormsby said.

"I think the prosecutor should come to it first," Mason said.

"Very well," Ormsby said, "perhaps the point is well taken. I will ask you, did you have an opportunity to see the persons who were conversing?"

"Not right then, but a few seconds later I did.'"

"Who were they?"

"The defendants in this case, Vivian Carson and Morley Eden."

"And where were they conversing?"

"In the living room."

"And you could hear them at the swimming pool?"

"Yes. The sliding glass doors were open, and it was possible to hear them very distinctly."

"And what did you hear them say? What conversation did you hear?"

"The woman said—"

"Now, by the woman, whom do you mean?"

"The defendant Vivian Carson."

"All right, what did Mrs. Carson say?"

"She said, 'Darling, we can never live this down.'"

"And then what? Go on, what was the conversation?"

"Then Morley Eden said, 'We don't have to. We'll never say anything about this to anyone. We'll let the newspaper people discover the body. Mason has arranged for a press conference out here later on. The reporters will discover the body. I'll pretend it's all news to me.'

"Then Vivian Carson said, 'But what about the knife? That's the knife from my kitchen,' and Morley Eden said, 'We can get another one. We're not going to let a thing like this come between us now. We have just discovered each other and we're entitled to happiness without having anything mar it. I'll fight for our happiness.'"

"Then what?"

"Then I heard them moving. I thought they were coming toward the swimming pool. I hesitated for a moment, then crowded in close to the edge of the building where they couldn't see me unless they came out on the patio and looked around."

"Then what?"

"Then I heard a door close and realized they had gone out. After that, everything was silent in the house."

"So what did you do then?"

"I went back down to the trail and climbed slowly and laboriously back up the hill to where I had left my car and drove home."

"What time did you get home?"

"About . . . Oh, I guess it was a little after eleven-thirty."

"And what did you do?"

"I didn't notify the police. I didn't know what had happened. I did feel afraid and—well, I felt guilty about spying and about eavesdropping. I didn't *know* that a murder had been committed."

"Now then, I will go back and ask you once more," Ormsby said. "Did you recognize the nude woman who ran and jumped in the swimming pool?"

"I think I did."

"If you could avoid the use of the word 'think" it would help," Ormsby said, "because that is susceptible of several interpretations and of course counsel on the other side will try to use the interpretation that is most disadvantageous to you. Now, kindly tell us just what your mental appraisal of the situation is."

"Well, I . . . I saw this woman. She was completely nude. I had of course only a fleeting glimpse but I . . ."

"Do you know who she is?"

"I feel almost positive that it was the defendant Vivian Carson."

Ormsby turned to Mason with a smile. "Cross-examine, Counselor."

"*Almost* certain?" Mason asked the witness.

She nodded.

"You aren't entirely certain?"

"No."

"You can't swear to it?"

"No."

"There's at least a reasonable doubt in your mind as to whether it was the defendant you saw or not?"

"Yes—I suppose it's only fair to say that there is such a reasonable doubt. I'm just not certain, that's all."

"What did you do when you got home?" Mason asked.

"I took a shower."

"Any particular reason?"

"No. I . . . Well, I'd been running around through the brush and the ground was dry. I was covered with dust. I wanted a shower and I took a shower."

"You had a visitor while you were taking the shower?"

"That was just afterward. Are you trying to have me tell about *your* visit, Mr. Mason?"

164

"I'm trying to get you to tell the truth," Mason said. "Did you have a visitor?"

"Yes."

"Who was he?"

"You."

"And did you have some conversation with me?"

"Just a moment," Ormsby said. "I object to this as incompetent, irrelevant and immaterial and not proper cross-examination. It has not been inquired into on direct examination."

"But there's no question about the conversation, is there, Mr. Prosecutor?" Judge Fisk asked impatiently.

"I don't know. There may be. I can't tell."

"The conversation," Mason said, "is for the purpose of showing that the witness, even at that time, was concealing certain matters and dissembling as to others."

"She was under no obligation to tell *you* what she had seen," Ormsby said.

Judge Fisk looked up at the clock. "Well, we'll come back to it after a brief noon adjournment," he said. "It is now slightly after twelve. Court will adjourn until one-fifteen this afternoon. During that time the jurors are admonished not to form or express any opinion as to the merits of this case, or as to the guilt or innocence of the defendants or either of them. Nor are they to discuss the case among themselves, nor suffer anyone to discuss it in their presence. Court will take a recess until one-fifteen P.M."

As the spectators filed from the courtroom Mason swung around in his swivel chair to face his clients. He motioned the officers out of earshot, signifying that he wanted a moment's private conference.

"Look here," Mason said in a low voice, "you're going to have to tell me what happened."

Morley Eden doggedly shook his head.

Vivian Carson blinked back tears.

"Let's take things up specifically," Mason said. "Did you or did you not park Loring Carson's car in your garage? Is that woman mistaken on her identification? If she *isn't* telling the truth the possibilities that are opened up are enormous. If she *is* telling the truth I

165

don't want to waste time and money trying to find the people who actually were parking the car."

After a moment Eden said, "I'll tell you this much, Mr. Mason. She's telling the truth. We parked the car."

"Why in heaven's name did you do that?" Mason asked angrily.

"If you knew all the facts," Eden said, "you'd realize there was nothing else we could do, but if you knew all the facts you wouldn't—well, you wouldn't give us a whisper of a chance."

"You don't stand much more than that now," Mason observed thoughtfully.

"We can't help it. We're going to have to fight it out along these lines."'

"Why did you park the car in the garage?" Mason asked.

"Because," Eden said, "it had been parked at the curb in front of Vivian's apartment, it had been parked in front of a fireplug and had been tagged. We only had a minute in which to act and we didn't know what else to do. We wanted to get it off the street."

"That car had been tagged for parking by a fireplug in front of Vivian's apartment?" Mason asked incredulously.

"That's right."

"And you knew, of course, that it was Loring Carson's car," Mason said.

"Certainly. And the worst of it is, it had been tagged for parking there at three o'clock in the morning. You know what that means—everyone would have felt certain Loring and I had resumed marital relations.

"I don't get it," Mason said. "But it's better to have people think you had resumed marital relations than to buy yourself a one-way ticket to the gas chamber."

"Of course," she said impatiently, "we know that *now*. But you have to think of the way we saw things on March fifteenth."

"Why did he park his car there?" Mason asked.

"I don't know, but I'm satisfied it was part of some diabolical scheme that Loring had been hatching up. He took his car and left it parked at the curb in front of the fireplug where he knew it would be tagged."

"What were you doing in town together?" Mason asked.

Morley Eden looked questioningly at Vivian. She shook her head.

"I'm sorry," Eden said. "We've answered all the questions we're going to answer, Mason. You've just got to carry on as a lawyer. Just assume that we are guilty. Let's assume that we committed a cold-blooded murder and you're the attorney representing us. As an attorney you'd look for every possible loophole in the evidence. You'd try everything you could. Now you just go ahead and try the case that way. Do the best you can. It's all we can expect."

"Damn it!" Mason said. "Are you trying to force your way into the death cell?"

"We're not trying anything of the sort," Eden said impatiently, "but if we are convicted, that's all there is to it. If we aren't convicted we've got to hold our heads up in society and live normal lives as well as we can. I'll tell you this much: We didn't kill him, and that's all we're going to tell you."

Mason said, "What time did you get to your house out there—that is, if you were in town together?"

Eden shook his head. "We've told you all we're going to tell you."

The deputies standing impatiently waiting for their prisoners moved in a little closer.

Mason shrugged his shoulders. "All right," he said, "take them."

Chapter Fourteen

MASON, Della Street and Paul Drake had lunch near the Hall of Justice at a small Italian restaurant where the proprietor had reserved a private dining room for them.

"I thought you said it was all circumstantial evidence, Perry," Drake said.

"I thought it was," Mason told him. "There's something about this case that simply doesn't make sense."

"Well, we've done all we can," Drake said.

Della Street said reassuringly, "You're doing a wonderful job, Chief. After all, if they expect you to go it blind you've got to just play it by ear. You've taken the sting out of a good deal of their evidence."

"But how am I going to take the sting out of Nadine Palmer's evidence?" Mason asked.

"Do you think she's telling the truth?"

"I don't know."

"Suppose you knew your clients were guilty. What would you do?" Drake asked. "You'd try to discredit Nadine Palmer, wouldn't you?"

"It's my duty to try and discredit her anyway," Mason said. "After all, she's given damaging testimony and it's up to me to use a searching cross-examination in probing for some weak point in her story.

"There's one thing I wish you'd do, Paul."

"What?"

"Get Della Street's fingerprints."

"Get what?" Della asked.

"Get Della Street's fingerprints," Mason said, his eyes on Paul.

"Well, that's easy," Drake said, grinning. "Provided Della doesn't raise any objection."

"What in the world do you want *my* fingerprints for?" Della asked.

Mason grinned. "I just thought I'd use them in cross-examination."

"Why?"

"Well, it might have a dramatic effect on the jury."

"When do you want them?"

"Right after lunch," Mason said. "Drake had better take you up to his office where no one will see him. Get her fingerprints, Paul, and mark the sheet of paper on which the fingerprints are made—use one of the standard sheets of fingerprint paper—and come to think of it, Paul, don't use all of Della's fingerprints. Take your secretary's and alternate fingerprints; one of Della's, one of your secretary's. Start with Della's little finger, take your secretary's ring finger. Get Della's middle finger, then your secretary's index finger; then Della Street's thumb."

"What in the world are you planning?" Drake asked.

"I don't know," Mason said, "but the way I look at law an attorney has a right to cross-examine a witness in order to find out if that witness is telling the truth. If the witness isn't, he doesn't need to lay a trap simply by asking questions. He has a reasonable amount of leeway."

Drake said, "I don't like this, Perry. You could get into trouble, particularly when you start mixing fingerprints."

Mason looked at him somberly. "Hell, I'm in trouble already, Paul. My clients are mixed in this thing up to their eyebrows and I don't know just where to strike. Anything I do may be the wrong thing."

"Well, this certainly looks wrong," Drake said. "It's no crime to take anyone's fingerprints but once you start mixing up the fingerprints of two people to deceive someone, you . . . Suppose they catch you, Perry?"

"That's the point," Mason said. "I don't want them to catch me."

"Quit worrying about it, Paul," Della Street said. "Let's hurry through lunch and get going."

Drake sighed. "The things a private detective has to go through when he's working for Perry Mason," he said lugubriously. "All of a sudden I've lost my appetite."

169

Chapter Fifteen

AT ONE-FIFTEEN when court reconvened, Judge Fisk said, "Mrs. Nadine Palmer was on the stand. Will you return to the stand, please, Mrs. Palmer?

"Go ahead with your cross-examination, Mr. Mason."

Mason waited until Nadine Palmer had seated herself and was glaring at him defiantly as though daring him to do his worst.

"This woman that you saw in the swimming pool," Mason said, "you glimpsed very briefly?"

"I saw her for some period of time, but she was moving very rapidly."

"The only time you saw her face was when she was running toward the swimming pool, is that right?"

"That's the only time I would have had a good look at her face."

"You say you *would* have had a good look at her face —meaning that you would have had a good look at her face if you could have kept your eyes focused on it?"

"Well, she was moving very rapidly and I had a little trouble getting the binoculars . . . Well, I saw her."

"And then you saw her jump in the water, swim across to the other side of the pool, bend over the hidden receptacle, and all that time she had her back to you."

"From the time she got out of the pool, yes."

"And while she was in the pool her face was under water."

"Yes."

"Now," Mason said, "when I called on you, your hair was wet."

"I had been in a shower."

"Do you usually wet your hair when you're taking a shower?"

"Sometimes. I intended to have my hair done the next day so I was careless about it."

"You remember that I asked you for a cigarette and you told me to help myself out of your purse or handbag?"

"Yes."

"Then when I opened it to take out a cigarette you came dashing out of the bedroom with a negligee wide open and trailing behind you. You were careless of the amount of exposure because of your haste."

"I wanted to help you. I was being hospitable and I thought you were a gentleman."

"And you whipped out a package of cigarettes and handed them to me?" Mason asked.

"Yes."

"Now, you're under oath," Mason said. "Did you get those cigarettes from your handbag or did you have them in your hand when you came running out of the bedroom?"

"I had them in my hand, actually."

"And the reason you were so anxious to get a cigarette into my hands before I reached one out of the bag is because you realized that the cigarettes in your bag were soaking wet, due to the fact that you had been in the swimming pool in your panties and bra and had taken your underthings off while they were wet and put them in the bag?"

"I object," Ormsby said. "This is not proper cross-examination. It assumes facts not in evidence and covers matters which were not covered on direct examination."

"I think I have the right to ask the question," Mason said. "I think it goes to the bias of the witness."

Judge Fisk regarded the witness thoughtfully. "I'm going to let the witness answer that question," he said. "I'm interested in the answer myself."

She said, "I suddenly decided that I didn't care to have you prowling around among my personal belongings, Mr. Mason. I thought I would bring you a cigarette so you wouldn't have to get one out of my bag."

"You're not answering the question," Mason said. "Were your actions due to the fact you knew the cigarettes in the bag were wet because you had put your wet underthings in there?"

She hesitated a moment, then looked at him defiantly. "No!" she said, spitting out the word with dramatic vehemence.

Mason said, "I talked with you for a while and you accepted a ride with me, did you not?"

"Yes."

"And while we were riding I mentioned the fact that Loring Carson was supposed to have had a girl friend in Las Vegas?"

"Yes."

"And you immediately asked me to let you out of the car at the first available opportunity. You wanted to be where you could get a cab just as soon as possible. Is that right?"

"That's right."

"And I let you out?"

"Yes."

"And you took a cab?"

"Yes."

"Where did you go in that cab?"

"Objected to as not proper cross-examination, calling for evidence which was not adduced on direct examination," Ormsby said.

"I'm overruling the objection," Judge Fisk said, "on the theory that this entire line of examination goes to possible bias on the part of the witness."

"I had it take me to the airport."

"Very well," Mason said. "Now, let me ask you something else. When you went to Las Vegas did you take with you a quantity of negotiable securities made out in the name of A. B. L. Seymour and endorsed in blank by Mr. Seymour?"

"No."

"Did you notice when you got to the Eden house that the receptacle was open?"

"Yes."

"Did you go to that receptacle?"

"No."

"Did you touch the receptacle?"

"No."

"Did you take any securities from that receptacle?"

"No."

"I submit," Mason said, "that *you* were the woman who dashed out of the house and into the swimming pool and swam across to the receptacle. I submit that you were not in the nude but that you were wearing your panties and bra; that you looted the receptacle of its securities, then swam back to get your clothes, taking off your wet underthings, wringing what water you could from them and putting them in your handbag."

"I did nothing of the sort."

"Did you," Mason asked, "take any securities of any sort to Las Vegas with you?"

"No."

Mason said, "I am going to show you a briefcase marked 'P. MASON' in gilt letters, and previously introduced in evidence as one of the People's Exhibits, and ask you if you ever saw that briefcase before this trial started."

"No."

"Did you take it to Las Vegas with you?"

"No."

"Did you arrange to have it surreptitiously put in my room in Las Vegas?"

"Oh, Your Honor," Ormsby said, "this certainly has gone far enough afield. This is not proper cross-examination, and I resent the making of an accusation of this sort where there is absolutely no evidence to support it."

Judge Fisk paused to give the matter thoughtful consideration. Then he said, "It is nevertheless a vital question as far as the defense is concerned. It would certainly go to the bias or motivation of the witness and I am going to permit it on that ground. Answer the question."

"No," she said.

Mason walked over to the counsel table and extended his hand to Della Street.

She handed him an envelope which Paul Drake had brought to court with him.

Mason approached the witness, dramatically opened the envelope, whipped open a sheet of paper divided into ten printed squares with an inked fingerprint in each square and said, "I am going to ask you whether these are your fingerprints."

"Just a moment, just a moment," Ormsby shouted, jumping to his feet. "I object to this procedure. This is completely irregular. Counsel has no right to make any such insinuation."

"What insinuation?" Mason asked.

"Insinuating that this young woman has had her fingerprints taken. I object to this."

"I will assure the Court, Counsel and the jurors," Mason said, "that there is no intent on my part to insinuate that these fingerprints were taken by any government agency. Quite the contrary. I am simply asking this witness if these are her fingerprints."

"That calls for a conclusion of the witness," Ormsby said, "and it is not proper cross-examination."

"I think it calls for a conclusion of the witness," Judge Fisk said, frowning at Mason.

"It is perfectly permissible to ask a witness if this is her signature," Mason said. "I am simply asking the witness if these are her fingerprints."

"But a witness can appraise a signature simply by looking at it," Judge Fisk said, "whereas in the matter of fingerprints it is something which calls for a somewhat expert conclusion."

Mason said, "I'm simply trying to find out. I have no objection whatever to having the witness take her fingerprints, put them on a sheet of paper and then hand both sheets to the clerk of the court to be marked for identification. Then if it turns out these are not the fingerprints of the witness that is all there is to it."

"But why should we do any such thing as that?" Ormsby asked.

"Because I have a right to ask the witness whether or not certain fingerprints are hers. I can ask her if a certain signature is hers, and I can certainly ask her if certain fingerprints are hers."

"The matter is unique as far as my experience is concerned," Judge Fisk said. "However, I am inclined to suggest that before I rule on the question the witness have her fingerprints taken and the two sheets of paper be marked for identification. Then the Court will call in an impartial fingerprint expert to determine the question."

"That is quite all right with me," Mason said.

"May I ask the reason for this question?" Judge Fisk asked.

"I am trying to establish something which goes to the bias and credibility of this witness, Your Honor. I cannot explain it at this time because if I did it would be disclosing my plan of attack and the witness would promptly proceed to—"

"Very well, very well," Judge Fisk interrupted briskly. "After all, gentlemen, the jurors are present and I suggest that we have no more discussion on the subject. The Court will take a ten-minute recess. During that time the witness can have her fingerprints taken and the two pieces of paper can be marked for identification."

"I certainly see no reason for it," Ormsby said.

"I think we have gone into that sufficiently," Judge Fisk said. "I want to give the defense every atitude in the field of cross-examination. Under the circumstances of this case I feel that the defense is entitled to that much consideration. In fact, it is a part of my basic policy that in every case involving a serious accusation of felony I give the defense attorney every possible latitude in cross-examining the important witnesses.

"This witness is a key witness, Mr. Prosecutor, and I intend to let the defense have every opportunity to probe her story by every legitimate means."

"Very well," Ormsby said, "we're perfectly willing. Let Mason try all of his trickery, all of his ingenuity, all of his dramatics and—"

"That will do, Mr. Prosecutor," Judge Fisk interrupted. "This is no time to argue the case. The Court will take a ten-minute recess. At the end of that time the two documents can be introduced and marked for identification."

The courtroom was in a hubbub as Judge Fisk left the bench. Newspaper reporters crowded around Perry Mason asking him what he was trying to do, what his strategy was, where the fingerprints came from, how he had secured possession of them, what significance could be attached to them.

Mason parried all questions with a smiling, "No comment."

When court was reconvened an indignant deputy prosecutor was on his feet. "Your Honor," he said, "we have had this witness give her fingerprints to an expert from the sheriff's office, an expert who is abundantly qualified. It now appears that there is not the slightest resemblance between the fingerprints on this card presented by Perry Mason and the fingerprints of the witness, and I submit that Perry Mason must have known that at the time. I submit that he is guilty of misconduct in taking advantage of the procedure of the court and attempting to intimidate the witness and create a false impression with the jurors."

Mason said urbanely, "If the expert you quote is prepared to go on the stand and swear that these are not the same fingerprints I will be bound by his testimony. I will withdraw my question to the witness as to whether or not they are her fingerprints. I suggest that this cross-examination be interrupted so the expert can go on the stand."

"Very well," Ormsby said, seething with anger. "You may step down, Mrs. Palmer, and I'll call Hervey Lavar."

"Mr. Lavar is a fingerprint expert in the office of the district attorney?" Mason asked.

"In the sheriff's office."

"Very well," Mason said, "I will stipulate to Mr. Lavar's qualifications, and you may proceed with the interrogation."

"I hand you two pieces of paper bearing fingerprints," Ormsby said. "One of them is marked Number F-A, and one of them is marked for identification Number F-B."

"Yes, sir."

"I will ask you what the document F-B is, first."

"That is a set of fingerprints made from the fingers of the witness who was just on the stand, Mrs. Nadine Palmer."

"And what is F-A?"

"That is a set of fingerprints which was shown to the

witness by Mr. Mason, asking her if those were her fingerprints."

"Is there any similarity between any of the fingerprints on the card F-A and any of the fingerprints on the card F-B?"

"There is not."

"Were those fingerprints made by the same person?"

"They were not."

"Were any of those fingerprints on the card F-A the fingerprints of the person whose fingers made the prints on F-B?"

"No, sir."

"Did the witness, Nadine Palmer, make any of the fingerprints on the card F-A, or did any of those fingerprints come from her fingers?"

"No, sir."

"I have no further questions," Ormsby said.

"I will waive cross-examination at this time," Mason said. "I ask that both of the documents be marked as exhibits."

"The prosecution doesn't want them as exhibits in its case," Ormsby snapped.

"Then enter them as exhibits in the defendants' case," Mason said, waving his hand in a gesture of generosity, indicating his utter fairness in the matter. "Put them in as defendants' exhibit one and two."

"Very well," Judge Fisk said. "They may go in evidence as defendants' exhibit one and two. Now you will return to the stand, Mrs. Palmer, for further cross-examination."

"I have no further cross-examination," Mason said.

"Any redirect?" Judge Fisk asked.

"None."

"Very well, Mrs. Palmer, you are excused."

"That's the People's case," Ormsby said.

"Does the defense wish a recess?" Judge Fisk asked.

"The defense does not," Mason said. "The defense will call as its first and only witness Estelle Rankin."

"As your *only* witness?" Ormsby asked in surprise.

"As my only witness," Mason said. "I don't think I'll need any more."

Judge Fisk said, "Just a moment, gentlemen. There will be no asides, please. Miss Rankin, will you take the stand, please?"

Estelle Rankin, a tall, well-formed redhead with large brown eyes, took the stand, crossed her knees, glanced at the jurors, then turned toward Perry Mason.

"Where do you live, Miss Rankin?"

"Las Vegas, Nevada."

"Did you live there on the fifteenth of March of this year?"

"I did."

"What was your occupation?"

"I worked evenings running a gift shop."

"Can you tell us something of the merchandise handled by that gift shop?"

"Ornate leather goods, curios, a small line of toilet accessories, postcards of various sorts, souvenirs of Las Vegas, and a line of magazines and cigars and cigarettes. Also a certain amount of luggage."

"On the evening of March fifteenth did you receive an order from a bellboy for a briefcase?"

"From the bell captain, yes, sir."

"What time was that?"

"It was nine forty-five in the evening."

"Would you know that briefcase if you saw it again?"

"Yes."

Mason said, "I call your attention to the People's Exhibit 26-A and ask you if you have ever seen that briefcase before."

The witness took the briefcase, turned it over in her hands and said, "Yes. That is the briefcase that I sold at that time."

"And up to the hour of nine forty-five on the evening of March fifteenth that briefcase had been in the stock of the curio shop and general store where you were working?"

"Yes, sir."

"You're positive."

"Positive."

"That's all," Mason said. "Cross-examine."

Ormsby arose with something of a sneer. "As far as

you know, Miss Rankin, this briefcase, People's Exhibit 26-A, could have been ordered by Mr. Mason that night simply for the purpose of confusing the police. The negotiable instruments which were found in it by the police could well have been taken by Mr. Mason from another briefcase."

"Objected to," Mason said, "on the ground it calls for conclusion of the witness. The prosecution purported to show that this particular briefcase with negotiable securities was brought by me from Los Angeles. I have a right to show where it came from."

"But that evidence doesn't mean a thing," Ormsby said. "It was merely an assumption by a witness."

"I suggest," Mason said, "Counsel can argue the case to the jury, and I submit that it does mean a great deal because I was being shadowed while I was in Las Vegas by a member of the Las Vegas Police Department."

"There's nothing in the evidence to show that," Ormsby said. "And anyway the point is immaterial."

"Well, then I'd like to recall Lieutenant Tragg for further cross-examination and establish that I was under constant surveillance," Mason said.

"My case is closed. You can't reopen it to cross-examine a witness now," Ormsby protested.

"Very well," Mason said affably. "I have such complete confidence in the integrity of Lieutenant Tragg I'll call him as my witness."

Lieutenant Tragg came forward, puzzled.

Mason said, "Referring you to People's Exhibit 26-A, Lieutenant Tragg, the briefcase which was found in my room. Who found that briefcase?"

"I did."

"Did you notice any other briefcase in the room?"

"No, sir, I didn't. But there was a suitcase in the room."

"I'm talking about a briefcase," Mason said. "Was there any other briefcase in the room?"

"Not in plain sight."

"Well, you went in there for a purpose, didn't you, Lieutenant?"

"Yes, sir."

"You were accompanied by Sergeant Elias Camp of the Las Vegas Police force?"

"Yes, sir."

"And, to your knowledge, was I being shadowed at the time?"

"There was a plainclothes officer detailed to keep a watch on you."

"And you had threatened to get a search warrant to search my room?"

"Yes, sir."

"For what purpose?"

"To look for a briefcase containing securities."

"And you found a briefcase containing securities?"

"I did."

"And was there any other briefcase in that room, either containing securities or from which securities could have been transferred to this briefcase?"

"I . . . I confess that I don't know," Lieutenant Tragg said.

"Why don't you know?"

"Because I went there to find a briefcase containing securities and when I found what I was looking for I discontinued any further search."

"Therefore," Mason said, "as far as you know, and to the best of your knowledge, this briefcase, Exhibit 26-A, was the only briefcase in the room."

"Yes, sir."

"Did you," Mason asked, "make any attempt to develop latent fingerprints on this briefcase, Exhibit 26-A?"

"We did. Yes, sir."

"Did you find any latent fingerprints?"

"Yes. We found some of yours and some of a person who could not be identified at the moment. I assume now they may have been the fingerprints of Miss Estelle Rankin, who just left the stand."

"Do you have those photographs of the latent fingerprints with you?" Mason asked.

"I have them in my briefcase."

Tragg produced the photographs.

"I wish to introduce these photographs as defendants'

exhibits three and four," Mason said, "and I have no further questions of this witness."

"No questions," Ormsby said.

"You're excused," Mason said, and turned to the startled prosecutor. "That constitutes the defendants' case, if the Court please. We have no further witnesses."

Judge Fisk was as surprised as Ormsby. "You wish to argue the matter now?"

"We're ready to proceed with argument right now," Ormsby said defiantly.

"So am I," Mason said.

"Very well," Judge Fisk said. "Proceed with the argument."

Ormsby walked forward to address the jurors.

"If it please the Court, and you, ladies and gentlemen of the jury, this is a peculiar case—an unusual case. It is a case involving deliberate, cold-blooded murder.

"The decedent may not have been the most perfect man on earth, but he was, nevertheless, entitled to his life. He was entitled to the protection of the law.

"The defendant Vivian Carson, finding her affection for him wearing thin, proceeded to divorce him. She felt that her husband had withheld certain securities, and it is quite possible that he had done so; in fact, the evidence would so indicate. I would be underestimating your intelligence if I tried to argue otherwise.

"That, in part, furnished the motive for the murder; that, and apparently a sudden infatuation between the to defendants. I was tempted to submit this case without argument, but I felt that I should point out certain facts to you members of the jury so that you will not be confused by any dramatic last-minute argument. I have a closing argument which will follow the defendants' argument, so I simply want to point out at this time that despite the attack which will doubtless be made on the credibility of the witness, Nadine Palmer, she has comported herself throughout in an admirable manner. She has told you frankly that while she is sure in her own mind the woman she saw jumping into the swimming pool was Vivian Carson, she is not going to make a positive identification. I think that is perhaps the best barometer of fairness that you could have in this witness.

"I submit that in view of the manner and demeanor of this witness anything that defense counsel may say, any attempt to smear this witness will be a boomerang which will damn the defendants.

"The defendants left their fingerprints on that hinged tile which covered the hidden receptacle. Those damning fingerprints, silent evidence that both of these defendants touched the *inside* surface of that tile.

"The testimony that their fingerprints were there is uncontradicted. You can see those fingerprints for yourselves. The photographs are in evidence. Just look at those enlarged photographs and reach your own conclusions. You don't have to qualify as an expert to tell when fingerprints such as these match. All you need is good eyesight and good judgment.

"The defendants had their hands on the *inside* of that tile, on the *inside* of that steel-lined receptacle.

"Why?

"Ask yourselves that question. No one has attempted to give you any reasonable explanation. There can be only one logical explanation. They murdered Loring Carson and took his hidden securities. They kept the cash. They wanted to transfer the securities. Their attorney, Perry Mason, had those stolen securities with him in Las Vegas.

"Was this a coincidence?

"Don't be naïve.

"Don't let Counsel pull the wool over your eyes.

"I ask a verdict of guilty of first-degree murder against both defendants."

Ormsby turned and walked back to his table.

Mason arose and smiled at the jurors.

"If it please the Court and you, ladies and gentlemen of the jury, I find myself at something of a disadvantage. The case against the defendants is predicated upon the testimony of one witness, Nadine Palmer.

"You have the assurance of the deputy prosecutor that Nadine Palmer is a reasonable, fair woman. Because she wouldn't identify the nude woman she saw jumping into the swimming pool as being Vivian Carson, you are told that this is an indication of her sincerity, a barometer of her integrity, and any attack on her will be a boomerang to the defense.

"The witness, Nadine Palmer, doesn't dare to come out and say that it was Vivian Carson she saw jumping in there because she knows it wasn't Vivian Carson and if it should turn out at a later date that the person she saw was actually someone else, she would then be guilty of perjury.

"So she hedges, she twists, she turns, she evades, she equivocates, and the district attorney's office wants you to take that as a barometer of honesty.

"If that's a barometer of honesty, then the barometer shows a pretty low pressure.

"Why didn't she have the integrity to come right out and say that she hadn't been able to recognize the person she saw, that she didn't know who it was, that she couldn't see her face. The sudden, startling apparition of this nude woman dashing out of the house and plunging into the swimming pool caught her entirely by surprise.

"You women on the jury will know how she felt. She saw this woman entirely unclad. The spectacle was one that startled her, and before she could gather her wits enough to take a good look the woman was in the swimming pool. After that she never saw the woman's face.

"But *did* she see a nude woman? *Did* she see anyone, or is she simply transposing her story so that she describes the part which she played in this case, and pretends that she was an impartial witness watching the event from a distance?

"Why didn't she go to the police with what she saw? Why did she rush home and take a shower, getting her hair all wet? Why were the cigarettes in her bag soggy? I'll tell you why. It was because she was the woman who jumped into the pool, swam over and got the securities and presently I'm going to prove it to you; and I'm going to prove it to you by your own senses and beyond any reasonable doubt.

"You ladies and gentlemen of the jury are mature people; you weren't born yesterday; you know the habits

183

of the police—when they have decided on a suspect, they marshal all the evidence indicating the guilt of that suspect, and all too frequently ignore evidence pointing to anyone else.

"I submit to you that the witness, Nadine Palmer, plunged in that swimming pool after she had learned the hiding place of the securities; that she put those securities in a plastic bag; that she started to swim back to get her clothes and found that Loring Carson had caught a glimpse of her as she jumped into the pool. Loring Carson ran back out of the house, and as Nadine Palmer tried to emerge from the swimming pool he grabbed her head and tried to hold her under water until she surrendered the bag of securities.

"How do we know this?

"Because *both* of Carson's shirt sleeves were wet to the elbow. He didn't get *both* arms wet opening the hinged tile. And when he reached for that hidden mechanism which raised the tile he did just what Lieutenant Tragg did when he reached for it. He did the only natural thing to do; he rolled up his right shirt sleeve.

"But even if he hadn't rolled up his sleeves he couldn't possibly have got his left arm wet reaching for that hidden release ring.

"The way he got *both* arms wet was by trying to grab a swimmer and hold her while she was in the pool. The swimmer got away from him.

"So what did Loring Carson do? He went into the house, found where she had left her clothes and stood guard over them, knowing that the swimmer wouldn't dare go out in public attired only in filmy wet underthings.

"And presently I am going to prove to you that this swimmer was not the mysterious nude Nadine Palmer says she saw, but was Nadine Palmer herself.

"She was trapped. So she quietly went into the kitchen side of the house, picked up a knife and, in her bare feet, walked gently and silently to the fence where Loring Carson was standing over her clothes and with his back to the fence, and plunged that knife into his body.

"That one act disposed of everything that stood in her way, stood between getting possession of the securities and having a fortune in her own name on the one hand or being apprehended as a culprit on the other.

"So then the witness, Nadine Palmer, plunged into the swimming pool, again went under the barbed-wire fence, returned to the pile of clothes she had left in the living room on the bedroom side of the house and, in the presence of the corpse, stripped herself of her wet underwear, put it in her purse, put on her outer garments and then, and not until then, retraced her steps up the hill to where she had left her car, carrying the stolen securities with her.

"After regaining possession of her car, she went back to her apartment and was changing her clothes when I arrived. She was panic-stricken, particularly when she realized she had inadvertently given me an opportunity to see that the cigarettes in her handbag were soaked with water.

"She suddenly realized that she had to do something to account for a period of financial transition. She had been a woman in modest circumstances, getting along on a small salary, and now suddenly she had blossomed into wealth. How could she account for this wealth?

"I mentioned Las Vegas and that gave her the idea she needed. She could go to Las Vegas and cut a wide swath at the gambling tables. People wouldn't know whether she was winning or losing over the long haul. Subsequently she could appear with this money and claim she had won it at the tables of Las Vegas.

"But she was too smart to bother with the securities because those could be traced, so what did she do? She put them in a briefcase, had the name 'P. MASON' stamped on the briefcase, took that briefcase to my room and planted it. Then she tipped off the authorities that I had a briefcase full of securities which had been given to me by my clients, the defendants in this case.

"Now, I can't prove that irrefutably and beyond all reasonable doubt because I am but one man; I am an attorney; I do not have the organization of the police, I do not have their facilities, I do not have their numbers, I cannot as an individual count on the cooperation of the Las Vegas police.

"However, if I can't prove it beyond all reasonable doubt, I can prove it to you to your satisfaction so that it will at least raise a reasonable doubt in your minds, and once I do that you must acquit the defendants. That is the law.

"You will notice in the exhibits in this case, exhibits of the briefcase containing certain latent fingerprints which the police say they were not able to identify. You will notice the photographic record of the fingerprints on the steel receptacle and on the lid of that receptacle that there are circled fingerprints which the police have determined, or at least they say they have determined, were the fingerprints of my clients.

"I am now going to ask you to take this fingerprint exhibit containing the known fingerprints of Nadine Palmer, fingerprints which have been testified to by the prosecution's expert as being her fingerprints, take those exhibits to the jury room and there compare the recorded fingerprints of Nadine Palmer with the fingerprints shown on those photographs which the police have not been able to identify; fingerprints which they say were badly smudged on the one hand, or could not be identified on the other.

"You don't need to be fingerprint experts to make this comparison. It is simply a question of looking for points of similarity. The police have shown you how this was done on the charts which were introduced showing the fingerprints of the defendants which were found on the lip of the tile—and of course the fingerprints of the defedants *were* found there. Why shouldn't they be? This was a house that was owned by the two defendants. Vivian Carson owned one-half, Morley Eden owned the other. What would you do if you returned to your house and suddenly found a tile in the swimming pool was actually the lid of a hidden receptacle? Wouldn't *you* wonder what had been put in there? Wouldn't *you* go and bend over it and inspect it?

"The prosecution has claimed to show you that those were the fingerprints of the defendants on that receptacle, *but they can't show you when they were made.*"

Mason paused dramatically. "They can't show you

186

whether they were made before the murder or afterward. They can't show you whether they were made before Loring Carson came to that house or not. They can't show you whether those fingerprints weren't made the night before when the defendants first discovered the hiding place of those securities and then waited to bait a trap for Loring Carson. By that simple act when Loring Carson came to that receptacle he could be apprehended and brought into court and forced to account for this fraudulently concealed community property, and be judged guilty of contempt because of the concealment of assets.

"Let's assume they tried that. Let's assume that something went wrong with their plan and suddenly, and to their consternation, they found Loring Carson murdered.

"Now then, ladies and gentlemen, I have here twelve magnifying glasses. I am going to leave these with the clerk of the court. The Court will instruct you that you are entitled to take the exhibits in this case with you and consider them in your deliberations. All I ask you to do is take these photographs and the undisputed fingerprints of the witness Nadine Palmer and—"

"Just a moment, just a moment," Ormsby shouted. "I assign these remarks as misconduct. The jurors can't constitute themselves as fingerprint experts. Fingerprinting is a science. It is something which only a competent observer can do.

"Now then, if there's any question about it we'll reopen the case and let the sheriff's fingerprint expert demonstrate that the fingerprints which the police couldn't identify are not identifiable; that they don't have enough points of similarity to identify them with the prints of anyone. We can't have these jurors going in and making a hit-and-miss comparison. Why, even a fingerprint expert can't tell from only a limited number of points of similarity whether—"

"Now, just a minute," Judge Fisk interrupted. "You've made your objection and your assignment of misconduct. The Court is inclined to think the situation is somewhat irregular, but the Court realizes that Mr. Mason is right, the jurors have the right to take these exhibits with them and I don't know that we can place any limitation on what the jurors do with those exhibits."

"Thank you, Your Honor," Mason said, and he turned to the jurors and bowed. "You will remember that the prosecutor himself has told you in his opening argument that all you need to compare fingerprints is good eyesight and good judgment.

"The Court will instruct you that if, after you have studied all of the evidence, there is a reasonable doubt in your mind as to the guilt of the defendants, you must acquit. I thank you."

Mason sat down.

Ormsby, on his feet, throwing caution and discretion to the winds, angry and enraged, shouted and bellowed at the jurors, pounded the table, pointed a finger of scorn at Mason, accused him of unprofessional practice, stated that he hadn't called a fingerprint expert to show that the fingerprints which hadn't been identified by the police were those of Nadine Palmer because he was afraid to.

Mason sat and smiled, first at Ormsby, then at the jurors. It was the smile of a man who can afford to be magnanimous in victory; a man who is watching the hysterical rantings of a person going down to defeat and knowing it.

The jurors were out two hours and a half, then returned a verdict finding both defendants not guilty.

Chapter Sixteen

PERRY MASON and Della Street sat with Morley Eden and Vivian Carson in the lawyer's private office.

"Now then," Mason said, "there's no one here except your lawyer, his secretary and the four walls of this office. You people are going to tell me what happened.

You've been acquitted of the murder. You can never be prosecuted for it again.

"In order to get you acquitted I had to throw suspicion on the principal witness for the prosecution. That was an part of my legitimate duties as an attorney representing you. I had to create a reasonable doubt in the minds of the jurors.

"However, I am not certain that Nadine Palmer murdered Loring Carson, and by George, you're going to help me find out who did. If she did, we're going to have her prosecuted and if she didn't we're going to see' that her name, which has been batted around plenty as it is, is not going to be besmirched any further.

"Now then, you two, start talking."

Eden looked at Vivian Carson.

She hung her head. "You tell him," she said.

"All right," Eren said, "here's what actually happened. And if you had known the facts, or if the police had found out the facts, we would have been convicted of first-degree murder without so much as a chance."

"All right," Mason said, "what happened?"

"From the first moment I saw Vivian Carson," Morley Eden said, "I was strongly attracted to her."

"It was mutual," Vivian Carson said. "This is a horrible confession for a woman to make, but I trembled like a leaf when I was around him."

Morley Eden put his arm around her, patted her shoulder.

"Go on," Mason said, "we'll start from there. It was love at first sight."

"Well, almost at first sight," Morley Eden said.

"In a bikini," Mason commented dryly.

"All right," she said, "I planned that deliberately. I wanted to arouse his attention. I wanted to get him—well, I wanted to get him to make some overt act so I could cite him for contempt and make him simply furious against Loring."

"All right," Mason said, "we'll take all that for granted. That's the way it started out. Now then, what happened after that?"

Morley Eden said, "On the evening of the fourteenth,

189

Vivian told me her car was in need of repairs. She asked me as a matter of neighborly accommodation if I would mind driving her down to a nearby garage and bringing her back.

"By that time we had begun to get fairly well acquainted and had made something of a joke about our so-called neighborly cooperation.

"I drove her to the garage, then she remembered something that she had forgotten to bring to the house. It was in her apartment. I told her I'd be glad to drive her to her apartment and bring her home. Then the question of dinner came up and I invited her to dinner. We went to dinner and after dinner went to a show. Then we went to her apartment to get the things she wanted, and while we were there we got to talking.

"She pointed out that this was what she called neutral ground and I said something about a fence and she said there was no fence between us here, and the next thing I knew I had her in my arms and—well, after that time passed rather rapidly. We started making plans, sitting there talking into the small hours of the night. I just didn't want to break the spell, and I don't think she did.

"And then suddenly we heard a key in the lock, the door opened and Loring Carson was standing there. He made some remarks that were decidedly insulting to his wife, remarks that were off-color and which were unbelievably coarse. I hit him. He got up and we had a fight. I threw him out of the door and told him if he ever came back or if he ever molested Vivian I'd kill him."

"Did anyone hear that?" Mason asked.

"Heavens, yes," Morley Eden said. "That's one of the things that bothered me. One of the neighbors heard the whole business, but that neighbor was sympathetic and evidently kept his mouth shut. I don't know why the police didn't suspect something like this and question the neighbors, but apparently they didn't have any idea that Vivian and I had been together in her apartment that night.

"The woman who saw us put the car in the garage volunteered the information to the police, but the police acted on the assumption we were both elsewhere during the night."

"Then what happened?" Mason asked.

"After I threw Carson out, we waited until daylight, then we had breakfast and went out. Loring Carson's car was parked in front of the fireplug and there was a tag on it.

"I decided it might be a good thing to move it so I took the brake off and pushed the car a little way down the hill so that it was away from the fireplug. When Carson barged into the apartment he had been drinking. Maybe he didn't know he'd parked in front of a fireplug. But Vivian thinks it was all deliberate—a last-ditch stand to avoid the fraud suit by creating evidence that would jeopardize the interlocutory judgment. Otherwise, why would he have a key to the apartment? Vivian certainly hadn't given him one."

"But what happened to him after he left the apartment?" Mason asked. "He must have driven up in his car. Why didn't he leave in it—after finding you two together there?"

"I don't know," Eden said. "That's one of the things that bothered me. We could look out of the apartment window and see the car parked there. I think perhaps I would have—well, we would have left before daylight if the car hadn't been there but . . . Well, that's the way it was. We thought he might have a gun and . . . well, we didn't know what would happen."

"Then what?" Mason asked.

"Then I came to your office and signed the verification on the complaint. While I was doing that, Vivian was seated in my car down in the parking lot. I couldn't help thinking what a surprise it would have been if you had known that."

Mason glanced at Della Street, nodded.

"We went home," Eden said, "and went in my side of the house. We saw a man lying there in the living room and ran down, it was the body of Loring Carson. He was lying there with a knife in his back, and he had evidently been stabbed by someone who had jabbed the knife into his back from the other side of the barbed-wire fence.

191

"It was a horrible predicament. Vivian recognized the knife as belonging to the set in the kitchen. And we had found the body together and we simply couldn't go to the police and tell them we had been out together—spent the night together—had trouble with Loring Carson, and then discovered his body.

"So I told Vivian that I'd drive her to her apartment and we'd hide Loring's car in her garage where it would be safe until dark, and then we'd leave it someplace where it could be found. Then I said I'd drive her up to the garage where her car was being repaired, that she could drive her car, that we could buy another knife to take the place of the knife that was missing from her kitchen and that I'd come out there to meet with the newspaper reporters at the time you had called the news conference, and that we'd all go into the house and that they could discover the body of Loring Carson at that time.

"I realize now it was a fool thing to do. We should have gone to the police and taken them into our confidence but . . . well, that's the way it was. After we'd once started covering up we could never have told the truth. No jury on earth would ever have believed us. It was up to you to take the case the way it was and go at it blind."

"I see," Mason said. "I—"

The telephone on Mason's desk jangled in a series of short sharp rings.

"That's Gertie's signal that Lieutenant Tragg is barging his way in and—"

The door opened and Tragg stood on the threshold.

"Well, well, well," he said, "I seem to be interrupting a conference."

"You not only seem to be, you are," Mason said.

"Well, that's too bad," Tragg said.

"And I may point out," Mason said, "that having been acquitted of the murder of Loring Carson, my clients are of no further interest to the police, so your inopportune entry is all the more inexcusable."

Tragg grinned and said, "Now, keep your shirt on,

Mason. Take it easy. My business is not with your clients, but with you."

"With me?"

"That's right," Tragg said, casually seating himself in a chair, tilting his hat on the back of his head and grinning amiably. "You've left us with something of a problem, Mason."

"What do you mean?"

"Well, there's a lot of newspaper pressure demanding that we go ahead and arrest Nadine Palmer but we haven't a case against her. You bamboozled the jury into turning your clients loose on the ground of reasonable doubt. In other words, you created a reasonable doubt in their minds that Nadine Palmer had done the job. But you can't prove it, and we can't prove it. That leaves us behind the eight ball."

"The district attorney," Mason said, "got into this thing without consulting me, and he can get out of it without my help."

"Quite right, quite right," Tragg said. "I thought you'd feel that way but, on the other hand, I just had an idea that you might want to cooperate with the police department; that is, not the department as a whole, but with Lieutenant Arthur Tragg as an individual."

Mason grinned. "Now that," he said, "puts it on something of a different basis."

Tragg said, "I'll buy your reasoning that we got a little bit off on those wet shirt sleeves. Come to think of it, a man as fastidious about his person appearance as Loring Carson would certainly have taken off his coat and rolled up his right shirt sleeve before he reached into the swimming pool to pull that ring and open the doorway to the concealed receptacle.

"Then I'll go a little further with your reasoning. He still had his coat off but he had rolled his sleeves down. He had completed his business with the secret receptacle. He went back into the house and was just about to put on his coat when he saw something that caused him to go running out into the patio, and at that time there was something that arrested his attention in the swimming pool. That, in all probability, was just what you thought

193

it was: a nude woman swimming back under the fence with a plastic bag containing the securities which had been lifted from the receptacle.

"Loring Carson bent down and grabbed her. He may have tried to hold her head under water, but he certainly grabbed her by the shoulders. He was struggling for the bag.

"She eluded him and swam back under the barbed-wire fence.

"Carson couldn't get over that fence, he couldn't get around it, and the only way he could have got underneath it would have been to have jumped into the swimming pool fully clothed.

"This solution didn't appeal to him but he had keys to both sides of the house so he ran out around the barbed-wire fence and into the other side of the house. The girl had her clothes in that side of the house and Carson thought that if he stood guard over the clothes the girl

"I don't want to be the fall guy in this thing,' Tragg there and got a knife in his back from the other side of the fence.

"Now then, I want some cooperation."

"What cooperation?" Mason asked.

"I don't want to be the fall guy in this thing," Tragg said. "Your clients have been acquitted. They can never be prosecuted again. I don't want them to confess if they're guilty, but if they are guilty I would like to have you tell me that I'd be wasting my time trying to pin the crime on somebody else. That will be a confidential communication which will never be broadcast, never be released to the press. It's simply a statement for my personal satisfaction."

"For your personal information," Mason said, "I would suggest that you continue your investigations, Lieutenant. I have every reason to believe that my clients are innocent. I'd stake my reputation on it."

"Well, now, that's something," Tragg said, his keen eyes sizing up Vivian Carson and Morley Eden. "Perhaps they'd tell me what actually did happen, just for my own guidance."

Mason shook his head. "They're not going to tell any-one their story," he said.

"Do you know it?" Tragg asked .

"I know it," Mason said, "and it isn't going to be told."

Tragg sighed.

Mason said, "There are a couple of fairly legible latents on that briefcase. Why don't you run them down?"

Tragg shook his head. "Of all the damn-fool things any attorney ever did," he said, "that business of making the jurors believe they were experts on fingerprints was— Why, do you know I found out what went on in the jury room. Every one of those twelve people hypnotized themselves into believing that two of the smudged latent fingerprints on that hinged tile were the fingerprints of Nadine Palmer, and that her fingerprint was on the brief-case. Of course, there *were* certain points of similarity. I think you can find about four or five. We don't consider we have good identification unless we have eleven points of similarity, but there was no way of getting *that* before the jury—not the way you handled the case—and when those jurors found four points of similarity they imme-diately became fingerprint experts . . . That was the damnedest thing anybody ever did."

"Well," Mason said, "the prosecutor brought it on himself. He told the jurors that there was nothing to this business of fingerprint comparison, that they could see for themselves, that they could take the exhibits into the jury room."

Tragg grinned. "For your private, confidential informa-tion, Perry, Morrison Ormsby is not the most popular deputy in the district attorney's office right at this mo-ment. In fact, there is a certain amount of hostility de-veloping toward him. I wouldn't doubt if he finds it ad-visable to go into private practice soon.

"Some of the newspaper reporters are getting the story from the jurors and they're going to make quite a play of it. We nearly always have latents which aren't iden-tified," Tragg went on. "If all defense attorneys could handle things the way you did we'd be in trouble all the

195

time. Of course, it was Ormsby's fault. But you baited the trap for him, and he walked right into it."

"There is one point," Mason said, "one which you may have overlooked."

"What's that?" Tragg asked.

"I never saw the briefcase which really contained the securities in my life until I saw it in the room and then I had this new briefcase sent in from the curio shop and put the old one in my suitcase. I had to do that so I could establish later on in court the time that I had received the briefcase; otherwise your witnesses would have claimed I carried those securities from Los Angeles; that I had received them from my clients and was taking them with me to get them discounted somewhere."

"I know, I know," Tragg said. "I tried to tell the Las Vegas police that you wouldn't have been that stupid but they wouldn't listen."

"All right, Tragg," Mason said, "I'm now going to get you the original briefcase that I found in my room. I think you may develop some latent fingerprints on that which may match the unidentified latent fingerprints you found on the lip of the receptacle there at the swimming pool."

"What the hell do you suppose I came up here for?" Tragg asked. "Of course we'll have to find the person who made the unidentified fingerprints. We'd have to have an identification of some sort, some standard of comparison."

"Exactly," Mason said. He went to the safe, took out a cellophane envelope containing the briefcase which had been left in his room at Las Vegas.

"Notice, Lieutenant," he said, "that this briefcase has gilt letters stamped on it reading 'P. MASON.'"

Tragg nodded.

"Rather an unusual way to mark a briefcase," Mason said. "One would mark it either 'Perry Mason' or simply with the initials 'P.M.' or perhaps with only the last name, 'Mason.'"

"Go ahead," Tragg said.

"Now, if you notice these letters carefully," Mason said, "the last part of the name seems to be a little more legible than the first two initials. In other words, this briefcase may originally have been marked with the initials 'P.M.' and then the last four letters were stamped on at a later date, the stamping being made so that the period at the end of the 'M' was obscured by the new letter 'a.' "

"Go on," Tragg said. "You're doing fine."

"Everybody seems to have overlooked the fact that Loring Carson had to have some way of getting out to the place where his body was found."

"Sure he did," Tragg said. "We didn't overlook that. That was elemental. He drove out in his car and your clients certainly took his car and drove it back to the garage under Vivian Carson's apartment.

"They intended to keep it there until night when they didn't stand quite so much chance of being picked up, and then take it out and leave it somewhere where it couldn't be traced to them."

"If they did that," Mason said, "why would they have taken the car to Vivian Carson's garage?"

"I'll admit," Tragg said, "that's one of the things that puzzles me."

Mason said, "Loring Carson came here from Las Vegas. He didn't come alone. Neither do I think he came with his girl friend, Genevieve Hyde. I think he had fallen for the Las Vegas system."

"What's that?" Tragg asked.

"When one begins to get a little tired of a hostess," Mason said, "another one cuts in. The one who is particularly adept at that in this case is a young woman by the name of Paulita Marchwell, and since her initials are 'P.M.' I wouldn't doubt in the least if that briefcase didn't belong to Paulita; if she hadn't gone to Los Angeles with Loring Carson or arranged a meeting here; if Carson hadn't left his car somewhere and had driven out to the house with Paulita. He told her to wait in the car. He wanted to put some securities in a place of concealment. He deliberately parked on Eden's side of the house in case Paulita got curious and started to nose around.

"He had retained keys to the house. He walked around

the fence to the side door, went inside and opened the lid.

"Paulita knew generally what was going to happen and what he was there for. All she needed was to find the place of concealment. She got into the Eden side of the house—probably through a window—stood where she could look out on the swimming pool and see what Carson was doing .

"The minute he deposited his securities and additional cash—I suspect it was a wad—and turned back into the house, Paulita stripped off her clothes and went like a flash into the water. She swam over to the receptacle, opened it, got out its contents and swam back under the fence."

"What was Carson doing all this time?" Tragg asked.

"Going out to the car, he found it empty and put two and two together. Paulita hoped it would take him long enough for her to get on her clothes and stroll casually from the side of the house, saying, 'Loring, dear, what a beautiful place. I was looking around. If you built this you certainly are to be complimented. It's a terrific job.'

"However, before she had a chance to do any of this Carson dashed through the front door and saw her running naked out of the swimming pool, carrying the plastic bag. He stripped off his coat and went after her. She ran back to the swimming pool and jumped in but Carson was able to grab her, perhaps by the hair. He reached for her neck, tried to hold her head under water,

"So then Carson stood wondering just what to do, put on his coat and stood guard over her clothes, feeling pretty certain she wouldn't dare run out onto the highway in the nude, and he had taken the keys when he left the car.

"She did better than that. She took a knife from the rack, tiptoed on bare feet, stuck the knife in his back, grabbed her clothes from under the fence, put them on, grabbed the car keys from his body, jumped in the car and took off.

"Then my clients entered the house. They found Carson's body and knew that they were in a terrific jam. In place of calling me and asking my advice then and there, they tried to concoct a story."

"A wonderful theory," Tragg said. "Would there be any way on earth it could be proved?"

Mason said, "You might ask Genevieve Hyde some questions. She went to Los Angeles by plane, I understand. It's barely possible she had a tip Paulita was stealing her boyfriend and decided to do a little investigating. She's closemouthed, but she won't lie. At least, I don't think she will.

"And put yourself in Loring's place. If the nude was not the girl who had driven him out there he'd have asked the girl who was waiting in the car to go in one side of the house while he went in the other and they'd have cornered this nude intruder.

"The fact he didn't play it that way is persuasive evidence that the nude was the young woman who had driven him out there in her car."

Tragg thought that over. "And Nadine Palmer?" he asked at length.

"Nadine Palmer did what any woman would have done," Mason said. "Having seen that receptacle, she wanted to find what was in it. She ran down the path from where the car was parked, but notice this, Tragg: the trail does not come in down below the barbed-wire fence; the trail comes in on the bedroom side of the house. In order to get over to the receptacle she simply slipped off her outer garments and dove in the pool, clad in bra and panties. She dove under the barbed-wire fence, found the receptacle was empty, went back, took off her underthings, squeezed out the water, put them in her purse, put on her dress and then heard voices as Morley Eden and Vivian Carson entered the house.

"She flattened herself against the wall, and from then on she's telling the truth as to what happened.

"Don't underestimate the intelligence of a jury. It really *was* one of her fingerprints that was on the lip of the receptacle."

Tragg shook his head. "We couldn't get enough points of identification to get a conviction."

Mason grinned. *"We* got enough points of similarity

to raise a reasonable doubt. But there were other unidentified latents. Try Paulita Marchwell."

Tragg thought things over, suddenly got to his feet.

"You've got a point," he said. "I think I'll go to Las Vegas."

Tragg left the office.

Morley Eden looked at Vivian.

"You see," Vivian said, "I knew we should have confided in Mr. Mason at the start."

Eden took out a checkbook. "I think," he said, "twenty-five thousand dollars would be about right as a fee in the case, Mason, and I'm going to penalize myself another twenty-five thousand for holding out on my attorney and forcing you to go at it blind."

Della Street cleared off a place on the desk for Eden's checkbook.

The three watched him as Eden wrote out a check: Pay to the order of Perry Mason—Fifty thousand dollars.